THE JOURNEYMAN

A BUILDER'S LIFE

Born in Crumlin, Dublin, in 1934, Billy French worked all his life as a bricklayer, eventually becoming an Inspector of Bricklaying in Local Government. He is also a novelist, poet, songwriter and playwright. He contributed to the best-selling *No Shoes in Summer* (Wolfhound) and wrote *Growing Up in Crumlin Village*. He has written many short stories for magazines and is a frequent guest on RTÉ radio. Billy teaches creative writing to young people on rehabilitation schemes and feels that, even after all the years, words still fascinate and surprise him.

This is an example of the terrible slums my father was born into in the Liberties in 1900.
(Courtesy of The Irish Historical Picture Company.)

THE JOURNEYMAN

A BUILDER'S LIFE

BILLY FRENCH

WOLFHOUND PRESS

Published in 2002 by
Wolfhound Press
An Imprint of Merlin Publishing
16 Upper Pembroke Street
Dublin 2
Ireland
Tel: + 353 1 676 4373
Fax: + 353 1 676 4368
publishing@merlin.ie
www.merlin-publishing.com

British Library Cataloguing in Publication Data
A catalogue record for this book is available from the British Library

ISBN 0-86327-901-5

5 4 3 2 1

Cover and Book Design by M & J Graphics
Printed by Cox & Wyman Ltd

I wish to dedicate this book to
Maeve, my wife and best friend for over 50 years,
and to my mother and father, who made me.

Contents

Chapter 1:	The Birth of a Brickie	1
Chapter 2:	Dublin Variety Shows	8
Chapter 3:	Jack Doyle in Dublin	19
Chapter 4:	Innocence Shattered	24
Chapter 5:	The Dublin Navvy	30
Chapter 6:	Building Boom	36
Chapter 7:	The Road of the Child	44
Chapter 8:	A Real Dublin Character	49
Chapter 9:	Marriage Discussed	56
Chapter 10:	McCarthy and the Embankment	63
Chapter 11:	The Magic of Kerry	73
Chapter 12:	Four Men with Funny Faces	83
Chapter 13:	Father and Son	91
Chapter 14:	The Unholy Talk in Church	100
Chapter 15:	The Killeen Years	108
Chapter 16:	The Death of My Father	123
Chapter 17:	Milking the Shovel	133

Chapter 18: Across the Pond 141

Chapter 19: My Time in Trinity 148

Chapter 20: A County Cow Brickie 156

Chapter 21: Wearing the Good Suit 162

Chapter 22: Inspector of Bricklaying 175

CHAPTER 1

The Birth of a Brickie

'Is that young fella there?' inquired the builder. As my mother nodded, he thrust five shillings into her hand. 'Tell him to get down as quick as he can to Granby Lane – it's off Parnell Square – and hire a hand-cart; then tell him to go to the M.R.C.B. shop in Lord Edward Street and pick up a few cans of paint – they have the order. When he's loaded it up onto the hand-cart, tell him to push it out to that address in Fairview, and tell him to hurry up – the bloody painters are standing out there waiting for the paint. Oh, and there's tuppence for his bus fare into town and back.'

With those somewhat scanty instructions, and with five and tuppence in my little hand, I began the journey of a journeyman that was to take and shape my life – the life of a Dublin brickie. Having made sure I had my lunch, a clean hankie and my manners – 'Don't forget your manners' – my mother sent me out into a world of strange creations and characters. The year was 1943.

Years later I heard of another boy recounting a similar experience with a hand-cart – only in his case, after seeing the said hand-cart piled high with ladders, planks and suchlike, and being told he had to push it out to Whitehall, he inquired somewhat sarcastically if the builder had forgotten anything; he was somewhat taken aback when the builder said, 'Now there's a good lad for reminding me; I nearly forgot the weights.' In those days, builders would not employ a man just to stand at the foot of an extension ladder; instead, large weights were attached to the ladder to stop it swaying. But this poor lad didn't know this and innocently asked a large red-haired boy who was working nearby, 'What are the weights for?' 'Oh, they're to tie around your kneecaps in case you break into a bloody trot,' replied this young lad without a smile.

Unfettered by such primitive restraints, and full of vigour, I leaped off the number 50 bus in D'Olier Street and ran as fast as my little fat legs would carry me, up O'Connell Street, into Parnell Street and across the Square, not stopping until I pulled up, sweating and puffing, in Granby Lane. Throwing the man in charge of the yard the two half-crowns, I quickly grabbed the two-wheeled vehicle he thrust into my hands and careered down O'Connell Street to the paint shop in Lord Edward Street. Having received my several large tins of paint, I very carefully put them in the front of the cart, checking I had the same number of tins as was listed on the docket. Having satisfied myself, and delighted that things were going so well, I placed myself between the two shafts and nonchalantly lifted them up.

It was then all hell broke loose. As I lifted the shafts, the weight, being all in the front, caused the hand-cart to tip up, leaving me hanging in mid-air. Then, as if it had a mind of its own, the hand-cart suddenly turned and took off down Fishamble Street with me clinging to it, my little fat legs going up and down like yo-yos.

'Oh, sweet Jaysus,' an old woman cried as she saw me dangling. 'The two legs is after being cut off the poor boy at the knees!' Then, just in the act of blessing herself, she uttered a terrible curse as she leaped over the tins of paint that were now hurling themselves out of the cart in every direction.

After what seemed a lifetime, the hand-cart came to a grinding halt outside a small second-hand shop. As I tried to pick myself up, a humpy old man with a beer-stained moustache poked his head out through the doorway. 'You can feck off with that,' said he. 'I don't buy bloody hand-carts, no matter what condition they're in.' Having stated his shop's policy in unambiguous terms, he moved stiffly backwards, banging the old door behind him.

Helped by passers-by, I gathered the tins of paint, now battered and twisted but still intact, and loaded them back onto the cart, this time making sure to place them nearer the back. Then, taking out the nice clean hanky that my mother had so carefully given to me that morning, I wiped the dirt and the tears from my face and limped out to the wilderness of far-off Fairview.

Arriving at the address, I expected a little sympathy; but none was forthcoming. 'You're late,' growled the foreman, a big man from the hills of Kerry. 'I was expecting you here ages ago.' Then he saw the battered tins of paint. 'Christ, man,' he muttered. 'We're working for one cute hoor: he's only after goin' and buyin' bloody tins of second-hand paint.'

1943 was a turbulent year that saw continued war and destruction around the globe, on land and sea. Battles raged in and around the Pacific, Russia and North Africa. In the vast Atlantic, many ships and men fell prey to the menacing U-boats, while innocent women and children died in the big cities of Germany and Great Britain as bombs were dropped from planes flying thousands of feet above them. All over the world millions of families were being torn apart or killed in this terrible World War. Here in Ireland, men and women were flocking in their thousands to join the many organisations and services that had been set up by Éamon de Valera's government because of the very real threat of an invasion by either Nazi Germany or Great Britain. But to a sixteen-year-old like me, 1943 was, as the song says, 'a very good year'. I was young, full of life and in long trousers.

After leaving school at the age of thirteen and a half, I followed my older brother John into a custard factory in the heart of what is now known as Temple Bar, the Left Bank of Dublin – God help us. In my time it was full of grubby old buildings owned by grubby little men, one of whom paid John and me the princely sum of nine shillings each for a forty-four-hour week. We each gave my mother seven and six, and another shilling went on bus fare, leaving us with the grand total of sixpence each. But there was some consolation: at least we had no money worries – not having any money to worry about.

Then John left to study bricklaying in Bolton Street Tech. I carried on earning and counting my huge weekly wage; but after carrying sacks of flour up and down very steep stairs for a few months, I straightened up one day and took stock of my situation. I didn't seem to be going anywhere fast, nor did it appear that I would in the future – it seemed to me that my little legs had grown even shorter with all that running up and down those perpendicular stairs.

So, without even looking for the sack, I found myself another job in Dundrum, cleaning out hen-houses. The people I worked for had about fifty hens and grazed about fifteen cattle in a nearby field. I was paid one pound a week – 'A pound of what?' my father asked, when I told him what I had to do. Then he looked at me over his glasses and said in a low voice, 'Try not to bring any of your work home, son, especially on your boots.'

One morning I arrived at work, full of the joys of spring, only to discover that one of the hen-house doors was open and about twenty hens were free-ranging around the yard. As I hastened to round them up and return them to their hen-house, one very large rooster took exception to the tone of my voice, or perhaps to the fact that I was a Catholic – one can never really know with a rooster! Whatever the reason, he strutted and stared at me, then slowly and deliberately unfolded his large wings and took off in my direction like a shot out of a large gun. Now, I don't know if any of you have ever seen a very large and very angry rooster full of indignation and in sweeping flight; up to then, neither had I. Turning around as fast as any frightened fourteen-year-old would, I took off across the large concrete yard, not stopping until I had jumped the gate into the nearby field. Breathless and sore, I turned back: the rooster had, for reasons best known to himself, lost all interest in me and was slowly walking back to join his lady hen friends.

I was so relieved and delighted that at first I didn't hear the snorting, nor the noise of galloping hooves. Then, glancing up, I had just time to see a young bull with a very mean look bearing down on me before I again leaped the gate, this time in the opposite direction. This incident actually happened to me, but I know the more cynical among you will dismiss it as just another cock-and-bull story!

Not seeing much of a future in cleaning and collecting eggs, I ventured into Dublin town and the clothing industry, which in my opinion held great prospects for an intelligent young fellow like me. My new employer, I am delighted to say, thought the same way: he trusted me with a three-wheeled messenger boy's bike, which he allowed me to ride for forty-four hours a week, and generously offered me a pound a week, rising to twenty-five shillings if I kept the three wheels pumped and my saddle clean and did not attempt to join a trade union.

After the confinement of the factory and the yard, I loved the freedom of the open road, especially in summertime. The bloody winter was another story. My old-fashioned bicycle had no roof, window or wipers, with the result that the rain had a tendency to find its way down the front of your shirt and into the more intimate parts of your body. One day I was explaining my discomfort to a group of other young messenger boys, as we dossed around one of the many back streets near Trinity College, when one boy, who came fully equipped with a decrepit old face and a body to match, whispered in my weatherbeaten ear: 'The rain goin' down under your shirt isn't too bad. It's only when it freezes over – that's when you're in trouble, mate, real trouble. Take it from one who knows.' Looking at him more closely, I felt myself slowly backing away.

Finding the winter wet and the frosty roads hazardous, I hastily relinquished any thoughts of making a career out of the clothing industry. So one cold winter's day I garaged my trusty three-wheeled bike and hung up my bicycle clips for the last time before walking quickly away.

And walk I did – right into a big meat factory in Abbey Street whose main purpose in life was canning beef for England. Was this, then, my destiny – to become a first-class canning expert, then a master butcher, and finally the managing director of this beautiful meat factory? My youthful dreams stirred my very senses. I'll never know how the foreman knew of my secret dreams, but he must have: clearly wanting me to learn the meat business from the ground up, he handed me a large brush and a set of instructions which, when read slowly, stated, 'Clean the floor and keep it clean.'

They say that a lad needs guts to get on in life, and I'd agree with this up to a point; but when you have guts for your breakfast, dinner and tea, you begin to wonder how much more you can stomach. The butchers, working through the night skinning and dressing the meat for the canners, created a most unholy mess of cows' guts and bladders and other unmentionable parts of their defunct carcasses. These unwanted innards were supposed to end up in the bins provided, but the butchers, most of whom didn't know their bin from their bladder, always seemed to drop the nasty bits on the floor – with the result that every morning, before I even got a chance to hang up my coat, the foreman would invariably shout, 'Hey, you, clean up that mess and be quick about it!' He was a most forgetful man: in all the months I was there, not once did he call me 'sir', or even 'Billy'.

I think it was this unholy forgetfulness on his part that made me decide to leave the meat trade and become a bricklayer. Notwithstanding the fact that my eldest brother Johnny was already serving his apprenticeship, my father, who came from a long line of bricklayers and could never understand my wish to do something else with my life, received me as the prodigal son.

CHAPTER 2

Dublin Variety Shows

The Ancient Guild of Incorporated Brick and Stonelayers' Association was established in Dublin in 1670, by a Royal Charter of King Charles II, and its offices were based in the Guildhall in Cuffe Street. This building's imposing stone frontage stood through famine, insurrections and civil war; but our birthright was no match for the city planners, who had it demolished in the 1980s in order to widen the road. There now remain only two such Guildhalls in Dublin city: Taylor's Hall and the Merchant's Hall.

Until a few years ago, bricklaying was a closed trade; so when a boy began his apprenticeship he was bound by indenture to his father, who in turn became his master. I was apprenticed to my own father in a short ceremony during which we both had to hold lighted candles; at the end of my apprenticeship, six years later, these candles were ceremonially blown out. The agreement or indenture that I had to sign states 'that William French, of his own free Will and Accord, and with the consent of his Parents, doth put himself Apprentice to William French (his father) to learn his Art, and with him to dwell and serve until the full Term of Six Years... be fully completed and ended; during which Term, the said Apprentice his said Master faithfully shall serve, his Secrets keep, his Lawful Commands everywhere gladly do... He shall not waste the goods of his said Master... He shall not commit

Fornication not contract Matrimony... He shall not haunt or use Taverns, Ale-houses or Play-houses, nor absent himself from his Master's Service Day or Night.'

One of the vital things the apprentice has to learn is the most basic principle of bricklaying: how to bond brickwork – that is, how to arrange bricks in a definite pattern while at the same time maintaining the greatest possible strength. To do this, the apprentice must first know that the long face of the brick is called a stretcher and the short end is called a header. There are many bonds, but the most common one is the stretcher bond, where the face of the building consists entirely of stretchers. Then there's the English bond, where there are alternate courses of stretchers and headers in the wall. Another one is the Flemish bond, where stretchers and headers alternate in the same course. These rules of bond are universal, allowing you to travel the world – thus the term 'journeyman'.

That old saying that 'a tradesman is only as good as his tools' is as true today as it was on the day the saying was coined. In order to achieve the august title of journeyman bricklayer, a young apprentice requires, first and foremost, a brick trowel. This is the main and most-used tool in the bricklayer's bag; with it, he picks up the mortar and spreads it evenly to form a bed for the course of bricks he is about to lay. Trowels range from 9 to 15 inches in size and come in all shapes. To the layman, all trowels of the same size are identical; but a brickie will take more time and care over purchasing a trowel than many a woman would if she were choosing a hat for her daughter's wedding. It has to be a meeting of two minds; he has to get the right feel for it, and this is only done after taking up and discarding maybe six or more trowels. But when he has at last discovered the right one, he'll then carry it from the shop with loving care, often unwrapped. Myself, I was always happy with a short, broad blade, finding it handy when I had to cut a brick in two or take a skelp off a rough-cut brick.

Next, the apprentice will need a lump hammer or club hammer, a boaster – a wide chisel used for cutting brick and stone – a scutch hammer for trimming bricks and other materials, several more cold chisels of various sizes for cutting and enlarging openings, a small pointing trowel for putting sand and cement in joints for weathering, and a plumb-line and pins for keeping the bricks level and plumb. The pins must be of good steel and the line made of hemp, not too thick. If a line breaks, it is never just tied; it has to be spliced so as not to upset the plumb line. The apprentice also will need a plumb rule. Also, a brickie always carried a three-foot folding rule and a small boat level; these could be seen projecting from his side pocket, for we carried both of them as the cowboy in the old West carried his guns. They helped to set us apart.

Looking back, I realise I was lucky to have started my apprenticeship with a local firm, Hetherington Builders. If I had joined one of the bigger building firms like Murphy Bros or Cramptons, as I did later, I would only have learned my own trade; but, by being the youngest member of a small firm, and therefore the 'nipper', I quickly learned nearly every aspect of building from the ground up. Working with carpenters, plasterers, bricklayers, plumbers and electricians, and watching all-round men like Billy Young, Pat Callaghan and Paddy Brohoon dig and lay foundations, paths and sewerage pipes, I amassed first-hand knowledge that stayed with me from those formative years and was responsible for me eventually becoming one of the first Inspectors of Bricklaying in local government.

There was another aspect of being 'the nipper' that I liked, besides lighting the fire and making the tea, and that was going to the building providers to collect the many varied pieces required for the different trades and jobs. In those days there were three main suppliers: Baxendale's in Capel Street, Brook-Thomas's in Lower Abbey Street, and Dockrell's in George's Street. Sometimes, if I was collecting timber, cement pipes or suchlike, I had to hire a hand-cart, but I never minded that; I always enjoyed walking around town. For Dublin was, in those days, only a large town; and, with petrol rationed, one encountered very little traffic or trouble.

One of the first big jobs I worked on was the Balalaika Ballroom at the top of Parnell Square, not a stone's throw from the Bamba Hall, another famous dancing venue. For these were the great days of ballroom dancing, when complete strangers, clinging to each other, danced their way through foxtrots, quicksteps, tangos and slow waltzes before rejoining their respective partners. The site had originally been a very large garage, so a considerable amount of conversion had to be done – knocking down certain walls, laying sewerage pipes, installing toilets, re-roofing and laying the dance floor itself. This, incidentally, came from the old La Scala Ballroom, which in turn had become the Capital Stage and Picture House.

The builder, Mr Hetherington, was, in the words of the Dub, 'the heart of the roul' and a very good employer. He had hurt his knee, and sometimes I would have to meet him at the 50 bus terminal in D'Olier Street and walk very slowly with him up O'Connell Street and across Parnell Square to the Balalaika. As we crossed into Westmoreland Street, he would stop and have a word with a large black man who always seemed to be standing outside the old Ballast office. As they talked to each other, Mr Hetherington – or Wimbles, as we called him – would slip a half-crown into the big man's pocket. As we walked away, Wimbles would tell me the same story that he had told me a dozen times before.

'That was Cyclone Warren I was talking to,' he'd say. 'A

great heavyweight boxer, he was. Did I ever tell you about the night I saw him beat Battling Siki in the Capitol Cinema? That was a great fight. Do you know that Battling Siki had a cheetah? He used to keep him on a big chain…' Mr Hetherington would smile quietly, his mind going back to another time, while my own mind wandered as well. I'd be thinking of what my father had told me about big Cyclone Warren and how much help he gave the lads during the War of Independence – so much that, it is said, he became the first black man to receive a pension from the Free State government. But, many years before that, Cyclone had been not only a sparring partner but also an opponent of the great Jack Johnson, then heavyweight champion of the world; he went the distance with the great Johnson over ten rounds, in a no-decision contest, on US Independence Day in 1908. Cyclone Warren had also fought Mike McTigue in Dublin, and it was claimed that he was the first man to knock out the famous Wexford fighter Jem Roache.

As long as I knew him, Cyclone Warren always wore a large overcoat with a velvet collar and an unusual-coloured bowler hat, and he carried a small cane. Over the years he became a familiar figure on the streets of the city; one would often see him surrounded by a group of boxing fans, recounting the highlights of his long career in the ring. He died on 16 March 1951, aged seventy-four.

As the Balalaika Ballroom neared completion, many of the big bands of that era came in to rehearse. And I thought, is it any wonder that a lot of musicians died young – or did they only look dead? – sitting up there night after night in draughty old halls, blowing their musical brains out. Men like Phil Murtagh, Billy Watson and the famous Johnny Butler rehearsed at the Balalaika, and during the break, the men in the bands would send me out to one of the many 'huckster' shops for cakes. These shops were so called because one could find a 'husk' of bread, a piece of fish, a few dead flies and a wasp all on the one cracked plate displayed in the window. I remember well seeing two women being served one day. The first woman was getting a pint of loose milk, while the other woman asked for a pint of paraffin oil. Having served the two ladies, the woman behind the counter rubbed her hands on her jumper before reaching into the window tray and taking out the six cream-cakes I had asked for; she then proceeded to wrap them in the same dirty newspaper that had been under the oil can.

When the bands rehearsed in the Ballroom at lunchtime, a lot of girls from the nearby Granby sausage factory would come in for a dance or two with some of the young and not-so-young building workers. I remember one carpenter by the name of Bob Taylor; he had a lovely tenor voice and was a great favourite with all the young girls. Unfortunately I was not so gifted, in either the musical or the dancing field. I lacked a singing voice, and I found out that on the dance floor I had some form of Siamese-twin legs – wherever one of them went, the other one had to follow, at the same time. The net result of this was that I was completely lacking in basic rhythm and co-ordination, and could never master the delicate, intricate steps of ballroom dancing. Nevertheless, I still regret the passing of this very enjoyable and sensuous pastime where people of different backgrounds came in such intimate contact with one another as they danced slow waltzes or other dreamy musical numbers.

The rear entrance of the Ballroom led out into the lane where Dublin's own saint, Matt Talbot, had collapsed and died on his way to Mass in 1925. A makeshift altar had been erected by the people at the time; eighteen years on, young and old people still brought fresh flowers to that simple shrine and then bowed their heads in prayer. To the Dublin people, Matt will always be one of their very own saints. Born into abject poverty in 1856, he was drinking at the age of twelve; having secured a job on the docks, he then turned to gambling as well. It was only when he reached rock-bottom, having lost his job and his friends along the way, that he rediscovered God and joyfully embraced the Catholic faith that he had abandoned as a youngster. This, for Matt, meant giving nearly all his wages – he was at this time working in Martin's timber yard – to the poor and denying himself the basic comforts of life. When he died at the age of sixty-nine, it was discovered that, not only had he slept on a plank of wood, but he had encased his emaciated body in chains as a form of atonement for all the sins in this world. After his death, when these things and the good works of mercy that Matt had performed in his lifetime became known, the people of Dublin took him to their hearts as one of their own. And this allowed them, as Dubs, to embellish stories of this holy and saintly man. Stories that could have no possible basis in truth were told and retold.

A number of years after Matt Talbot died – according to one of the many stories I have heard from people on building sites – there was a move by the Catholic Church to start the slow process of beatification, which might eventually lead on to his canonisation. To this end, they searched Dublin for anyone who might have witnessed Matt Talbot working a miraculous cure by the laying on of hands. After a lot of exhaustive enquiries, they eventually found an old 'butty' or friend of Matt's who claimed to have witnessed such a miracle. Having dressed him up for the occasion, the clergy sent him off to Rome, where three old cardinals suitably clothed in ermine, their frosty eyes hidden behind thick glasses, sat stony-faced along one side of a large table. Doffing his cap, the old friend of Matt's was curtly invited to sit down opposite them.

'We were led to believe that you witnessed the laying on of hands by one Matt Talbot, and that as a result of this laying on of hands a miracle took place. Is that true?'

'Well – sorta,' the old man replied.

'Please explain it to us in your own words and in your own time.'

These apparently kind words from the nicest of the three churchmen seemed to relax the old man. 'Well, it was a very cold day in the winter of '24, and Matt and meself bein' on the dry –'

'On the dry? Please explain this expression.'

'We were both off the gargle – I mean the drink, your worships. And we were walkin' along Hume Street when out of the Cancer Hospital came this poor man – half his face was gone. Well, Matt takes pity on the poor frozen divil; and seein' that there was a lot of horse traffic in those days, Matt bent down and rubbed the hot horse shi– I mean manure – well into your man's face, your worships.'

'And was it a miracle? This laying on of hands?' asked one of the cardinals, leaning forward to catch the answer.

'It sure was,' the old man replied. 'It was a real miracle that this poor man's relations didn't lay hands on Matt. Although they did try to find him – they said they would smother him to death in the same horse shit.'

The person who told me this story believed that these events really took place; you can judge for yourself!

Around that time, I was sent on another 'small job' (according to Mr Hetherington, there was no such thing as a big job). There I, along with some older men, had the privilege of helping to carry out internal and external repairs to Noel Purcell's mother's house in Lower Mercer Street. Actually, she was the proud owner of two adjoining houses; one of these had been turned into a small shop, from which Mrs Purcell – who was then an elderly lady – ran her very successful antique business.

I was always very impressed, and highly delighted, when

Noel himself arrived to visit his mother. His arrival on an old bicycle – for these were the war years, and there was certainly no petrol for stars, no matter how big they were – always created a bit of local excitement. At that time Noel Purcell was one of the biggest stars we had in show business; apart from the fact that he was six foot four, he was also the biggest draw in one of the biggest theatres in Europe, namely the Theatre Royal.

In those uncertain days of World War II, we Dubliners were spoilt for choice when it came to real live entertainment. We had the Gaiety Theatre, where Jimmy O'Dea, Maureen Potter and Danny Cummins reigned supreme; at the Olympia one could see Jack Cruise and his company or Cecil Sheridan and Peggy Dell perform in their own individual ways, while over at the Queen's one had the Happy Gang, which included Bill Brady, Jimmy Harvey, Mick Eustace and Cecil Nash. Meanwhile, at the Capitol one could always view a first-rate film, after seeing Sean Mooney, Johnny Keys and funny man Jack Kerwin perform and watching the lovely Capitol dancing-girls going through their high-kicking routines. All the theatres had their own dancing-girls, and none were more famous then the Royalettes. Appearing with them in the Royal were Frankie Blowers, May Davitt and one Joseph McLoughlin, who soon became known as Josef Locke.

But no matter who came and went, Noel Purcell – with his appearances in revues and pantomimes where new scripts had to be learned and rehearsed each week – was the shining star who kept the Royal doors open through those six lean years of rationing and uncertainty. So meeting Noel himself, as I did a good few times, was an uplifting experience that has remained with me ever since. Surrounded by well-wishers, as he always was, he would dismount from his bicycle; then, catching my eye, he'd say in that authentic Dublin voice of his, 'How's it goin', me oul' brown son?' And I, being all of sixteen, would be secretly delighted that he had singled me out – completely unaware that, as I was standing in his mother's doorway and blocking his entry, what else could the good man do but say hello to the poor young gobshite framed in the door?

Noel was a religious man who always said his morning and night prayers and, no matter where he was in the world, always tried to visit a house of worship at least once a day. To explain this habit, he often recited a small poem:

Whenever I am near a church
I always pay a visit,
So the day that I am carried in
The Lord won't say, 'Who is it?'

Always interested in film, he went on to achieve great success in over fifty movies, including *Captain Boycott* with Stewart Granger, *Odd Man Out* with James Mason, *Moby Dick* with Gregory Peck, *Shake Hands with the Devil* with James Cagney and *Mutiny on the Bounty* with Marlon Brando and Peter O'Toole. A fellow Dub was once heard saying, 'The best in the world acted with our Noel.' He would have enjoyed that.

There's a large plaque inside the entrance of Whitefriars Church, on Dublin's Aungier Street, which reads:

'Tell the Gaffer Noel is ready.'

Noel Purcell spent his last weeks in the hospital he loved so well, the Adelaide; 'a grand hospital in the heart of auld Dublin' as he put it, says Father Tom McLoughlin, O.Carm., who is chaplain to the Adelaide. He knew the end was drawing near and made no secret about it. All through his illness his great faith was as big as his rugged physique. He regarded himself as waiting in the queue for 'going up above' and spoke jokingly of others getting in before him.

'One night when I came on duty,' recalls Father McLoughlin, 'a nurse told me that Mr Purcell was very anxious to see me. We chatted for a while. Then he riveted me with his big imploring eyes under the shock of white hair. "Father, would you do me a favour." He raised his arms heavenwards. "Would you tell the Gaffer that Purcell is ready when he is."'

On Sunday morning March 3 1985, the Gaffer, as he lovingly referred to the Lord, sent for him. His beloved wife Eileen and his sons were there to see him off. The queue had shortened, the waiting was over and Noel Purcell had a most peaceful death.

CHAPTER 3

Jack Doyle in Dublin

In the dark days of 1943, another shining star came to rest for a while in Dublin. His name was Jack Doyle, and by his side was his beautiful Mexican wife Movita. It is very hard to explain to young people today, brought up in an era that calls a mundane singer with one hit record a megastar, the effect Jack Doyle had on young and old – especially the ladies – in those grim grey days of the Second World War.

For although officially we as a nation were neutral, the fact was that thousands of our young men and women had crossed the pond to Great Britain to join the armed forces or to work in the factories, with the result that whole families had been broken up. Ageing parents suffered the loss of their teenage sons and daughters, and thousands of small children were deprived of their fathers, while others saw their older brothers and sisters leave, many never to return. It was also a time of severe rationing of tea, sugar, clothing and fuel. City buses stopped operating at 9.30pm, and, with very few taxis in evidence, one had to walk home from the dance hall or picture-house at night, knowing that rain-soaked clothes could not be dry for morning due to the lack of fires in many a grate. The result of all this was often tuberculosis, or TB, as it was called – a fearful, deadly disease that struck many families indiscriminately. Even though it was no respecter of class or rank, it was still looked upon as a social disease, perhaps because people wrongly believed that malnutrition was the chief cause; therefore the parents, in some strange way, felt their neglect had caused their children to contract it. Its victims were often shut away in a back room or a shed at the end of the garden and treated like lepers by their families and friends.

So it was against this background that the famous Jack Doyle arrived in our midst – and famous he was. Born in County Cork in 1913, he had gone on to join the British army and become not just a useful boxer, but the darling of the jet set, which at that time centred around His Royal Highness Prince Edward in London. But then America beckoned to Jack, and the six-foot-three young giant, with his dark curly hair and incredible good looks, soon appeared in several movies and became the toast of the film world. It was while in Hollywood that he met his future wife, Movita. Movita was a star, having acted in several films, including the original *Mutiny on the Bounty* with Clark Gable and Franchot Tone. After meeting the 'Gorgeous Gael', as Jack was called by the press, she left her career and family and followed him to England by way of Mexico, where they were married in a registry office.

Arriving back in Great Britain, Jack carried on his merry-go-round life of parties, drinking and gambling. In between he would put on the gloves and fight the bad fight – notably against the former British cruiserweight champion Eddie Phillips in the summer of 1939. That fight lasted less than one round; but after being counted out, the bold Jack, not realising that the fight was over, jumped up and waved to the many thousands of people, who stared back in silence.

But a more deadly fight was about to begin: the Second World War. According to Jack, he tried to re-enlist in the British army, but on being told he was only fit to dig ditches, he felt rather peeved and decided there and then that Dublin was the only place to be. But, of course, being Jack, he delayed his departure for a few years, arriving in Dublin in the winter of 1943.

The Ireland of those times was filled with bigots and small men, who effectively closed all doors on Jack and his beautiful wife and only opened them when Jack and Movita consented to be married once again, this time in St Andrew's Catholic church. Now that the Doyles were decent Irish Catholics like the rest of us, they were invited to top the bill at the big Theatre Royal in Dublin. This they did, playing to full houses for many weeks, until someone close to Jack told him he'd make a killing if he boxed again. His opponent was one Chris Cole, a useful heavyweight from Mullingar. The fight took place in Dalymount Park on a warm night in June and lasted less than one round. Needless to say, the spectators were stunned when Jack the Giant fell to his knees, and then, having been counted out, stood up, waved to a very angry crowd and left the ring smiling broadly.

It was the start of his downfall, in which he would lose not only his good looks, but his lovely wife as well. Soon after that she left him, eventually returning to Hollywood. There she married Marlon Brando, while the mighty Jack Doyle, having lost the one real love of his life, went rapidly downhill, existing in the back streets and lanes of Dublin.

I remember one morning, as I was going to work, I saw a crowd of people standing at the corner of Charles Street and became curious. Dismounting from my old bicycle, I edged nearer to find out what all the commotion was about – only to see an old man dressed in off-white long johns, his dirty bare feet flapping in the cold wind, uttering obscenities that could (and would) only be repeated in the confessional the following Saturday night.

It transpired that he was one of the many key-holders who resided in a large tenement house nearby. A lady of the night who occupied another room in the same house had, out of the goodness of her heart, brought the bold Jack home for a mug of cocoa. However, the cocoa had apparently been rather hot; it had taken poor Jack all night to drink it, the lady claimed.

But the flapper with the baldy napper was having none of this 'oul' codswallop', as he called it. 'It's bad enough havin' to live in this kip of a house without you makin' a hoor-house out of it!' he roared through toothless gums. Needless to say, this Joycean remark brought a cheer from the ever-growing crowd. Thus encouraged, the elderly man rolled up his sleeves and adopted the stance of a boxer as he shouted, 'Come on down, Doyle, and face me like a man!'

All eyes were now turned upwards to the top window as Jack Doyle's massive black head came into view. He raised a huge hand and waved to the crowd below, and we, loving the whole scenario, cheered all the more.

After the war ended, Jack returned to London to relive his former glory days, proving the old adage that 'you can't keep a good man down'.

These crowd gatherings were quite a feature when I was a youngster. I remember seeing another one as I cycled home one evening through New Street. A large group had gathered to listen to a shouting match between two Dublin women. One was perched in a window two stories up, while the other woman leaned out of a window that unfortunately happened to be situated on the ground floor of her house, thus giving the other lady an distinct advantage.

The row, having travelled the usual roads of drink, debauchery and lowly pedigree, was suddenly turned upside down when one of the women whispered the dreaded word 'TB'. Even for the most innocent onlooker, the mere mention of TB was considered to be below the belt. Tuberculosis is a very serious and infectious disease, and in the 30s and 40s, before the widespread use of penicillin and other wonder drugs, it was considered fatal. I myself knew of one family that lost four or five teenage children, boys and girls, to the disease, all within the space of a few years. My father always referred to their poor mother as 'the Mother of Sorrows'.

So when the woman in the lower window spit out the sinful word 'TB', the other woman rolled up her sleeves and announced in a voice that carried the length and breadth of New Street: 'Thank God, there never was and never will be TB in either side of my family!' This statement was greeted by the onlookers with loud cheers.

But as the shouts subsided, a little boy of about ten years of age appeared beside the woman. From where I was standing, I could see by his little face that he was trying to defuse the situation, for he cried out, 'Mammy, me daddy will be home soon for his tea.'

The effect of the son's words on the mother was mighty. She placed her two hands on her ample hips, and her voice was heard by all as she replied, 'Yes, son, your daddy will be home soon for his tea. And I'll tell you something else: he'll have tomatoes for his tea!'

This statement was greeted with even greater cheering. As the roars from the crowd increased, the other woman, knowing that she was beaten, conceded defeat by slamming shut her window. We, believing that the battle had been won by the better woman, turned for home, facing the wind and rain along the Grand Canal banks with lighter hearts.

CHAPTER 4

Innocence Shattered

In those far-off days of my apprenticeship, strange and sometimes downright weird people abounded in the trade – people with such names as 'Squabbler' (portrayed so well by the late Ray McNally in the film *My Left Foot*), 'Rise-a-Row', 'Jack-up', 'the Lumper', 'the Bishop', 'the Mouth' and many, many others of a more or less complimentary nature. My own grandfather, who was on the Executive Committee during the 1913 lock-out, answered to the strange name of 'Ha'-Pa'-Nine'. This was because he carried a pocket watch – I'm told it was a large turnip affair – which, of course, was frowned on by the builders of the day. When asked the time, my grandfather would make a big thing of opening his jacket, taking out the big watch and looking at it for as long as the foreman would allow. Then, returning the watch to his inside pocket, he would smile and declare, 'It's ha'-pa'-nine.'

When you think of the builders' constantly changing places of work and their total dependence on weather and other factors, it becomes clear that these names were not so much acquired as bestowed on them by their peers. These men, by the nature of their trade, had to work to set rules that were universal, so they tried to show their own individuality, in circumstances that were often far worse than those the male prisoners of the State have to endure today.

When I was young, my favourite nickname was that of a

bricklayer who was known as 'the Liar'. It was said he never, ever told the truth – not even in the confessional. He had served as a soldier in the First World War, and he was asked one day if he had won many decorations. Shaking his head, he replied, 'No. You see, when the other lads came home from France, they were met with bands, streamers and such-like; but, because I had been a prisoner of war, I wasn't released until well after all the shouting and celebrations had died down.' When at last he arrived back in Dublin, he claimed, there was no one there to meet or greet him. At that time, the Liar, like the rest of the working class, lived in a large old tenement house in the city. Coming up the street towards his home, he saw some of the women, his own wife among them, standing outside on the steps gossiping. Ashamed because he had not returned a hero, he made a dash for the stairs when their backs were turned – only to hear one of the women cry out, 'My God, there's the Angelus bell ringin' out and I haven't even the dinner on.'

'Only it wasn't the Angelus,' said the Liar; 'it was only the medals on me chest jangling.'

England, being the home of brickwork, was a Mecca for all Irish bricklayers, and the Liar was no exception. He was once asked by my father, 'What was the highest building you ever worked on?'

'I'd say it was in Liverpool,' replied the Liar. 'A church belfry, it was. Ten weeks I was on it; and, having completed it rather late one afternoon, I went home to my digs, had a wash and shave and went to the music hall. And lo and behold, about the fifth act I think it was, a notice was displayed on the stage: "Would the bricklayer who completed work on the belfry of the nearby church return immediately and remove the last three courses of brickwork, as the bloody moon wants to pass."'

Many years later, when I was an Inspector in local

government, I used to park my car opposite St Audoen's Flats in Cook Street, where the old Dublin wall was then being repaired and rebuilt to its former glory by some of Dublin's best stonemasons. These craftsmen's skills will ensure that their work will last another thousand years; for, like the Ten Commandments, their life's work is carved in stone. Chief among them was a Mr Hanly, a relation of the famous Liar. I always addressed him as Mr Hanly; and, although my father had passed away nearly forty years before, he invariably referred to me as 'Young French. He's a son of Billy French.' This was not really an introduction, more of an explanation for my presence – especially if I was wearing my good suit, which for some reason seemed to cause him embarrassment.

The massive wall was topped by rough-cut stone piers, fairly close together, which gave it the look of a battlement wall. One morning, as I got out of my car, I noticed Mr Hanly himself holding a large level on a long straight-edge taking in about ten of these piers. From the way he was peering at the level, I knew he should be wearing glasses due to his advanced years, but I also knew he wouldn't wear them while the young engineer was standing close by. Knowing from experience that, as the wall was so high, one could afford a three-inch differential that would not be seen from the ground, I shouted up as a joke, 'Mr Hanly, you're an eighth of a inch off in your levels!'

Without even looking down, he shouted, 'You'd know nothing about it, Young French – we're working to metric.'

As I have already stated, in 1943 I was sixteen years of age, with money in the pockets of my long trousers, and in love with the world. That was the happy frame of mind I was in when I was shifted from the Balalaika Ballroom to Gardiner Street. Mr Hetherington had secured the job of knocking down and rebuilding a large section of one of the many tenement houses that were in use in the Dublin of that period.

How could I have known then, when I was making that move, that I was about to lose my innocence, my youthful belief in all things good and wholesome?

These tenement buildings, as they were called, were really old Georgian houses that had survived well past their sell-by date. When the gentry moved out of their run-down town houses, the poor of Dublin moved into them *en masse.* Often there were five or six families in one building and eight or more in each family, all sharing one cold-water tap and one toilet, which was usually situated in the large back yard. Although the conditions were appalling, with the stench of urine invariably assailing your nostrils as you entered the hall, it has to be said that the vast majority of those who inhabited these tenements were God-fearing, decent, honest people – especially the women, who washed, cooked and tried to feed large families, often on a mere pittance. Unemployment was at an all-time high, and many men had to leave home to get work across the pond in England; it was left to the poor mothers to bring up the children in the love and fear of God, and this they did quite successfully.

In the tenement building we were repairing, there was one such young woman. She was the mother of two-year-old twins, a girl and a boy; like so many others, their daddy was away working in London. I, having a younger brother and sisters, got on well with the two children; when I'd go to the shops for the men I would sometimes buy them sweets, and occasionally I would give the little lad a jockey-back or a jaunt in the wheelbarrow. The young mother herself was very pretty, with long hair and brown eyes that twinkled when she laughed. The five men and I usually had our tea-break in her place, and if it was near twelve, she would stand and say the Angelus prayer out loud, thereby compelling the more reluctant among us to join in. To me, she symbolised all that was good in womanhood. She was my mother and sisters rolled into one.

Then, one Monday morning, I arrived early. I knocked, as I always did, and pushed the door open – only to discover this beautiful young mother in bed with a strange man. Their savage grunting and groaning, as they clung to each other and twisted in a fast, rhythmic motion, filled me with a sense of numbness – which probably came from the deep shock – followed almost immediately by hatred for the stranger and for this beautiful young woman whom, in my innocence, I had placed high upon a pure white pedestal. My anger, I told myself later, came from the fact that the two innocent young babies, as they played with their toys in a nearby bed, had also seen and heard what I had witnessed. But, without realising it, I too had lost my innocence as I saw for the first time my world of solid principles collapse around me.

Feeling as if I were in some terrible nightmare, I stumbled from the room, down the dark stairs and out into the back yard, where one of the men was already mixing the mortar to be used by the two brickies. I remember he called out to me – something about wetting the mortarboards – but I refused to hear him; my head was still filled with those terrible sounds I could not shut out. For the next few mornings I avoided all contact with the family by not going up to their room for my ten o'clock break; instead I brooded and sulked like a small boy who has seen his favourite toy taken from him and trampled into the dust. I had convinced myself that nothing could ever be the same again.

I suppose it's the price one pays for being born a boy. We were never encouraged or allowed to express our real feelings and emotions. You always had to climb as high as or higher than your pals, without regard to the fact that you were really frightened of heights; sometimes, when you dragged yourself to the river with the others for a swim, you wondered – as you dived off the bank into the icy unknown – whether any of them felt as frightened as you. Most men are able to share their recreational moments with their fellow men; but their feelings – those real, inner-self feelings... they bury them deep, like the proverbial dog with the bone. How could I even attempt to explain to anyone my deep hurt at what I'd witnessed, when I myself couldn't understand the very real hurt I was experiencing?

When I met the same lady on the stairs, a few days later, the silence between us was deafening. Trying to avoid her eyes, I swiftly bent down and, grasping the front wheels of the children's pram, helped her carry it down the stairs. As I turned to leave, I heard her say very, very softly, 'I'm truly sorry, Billy, you had to see what you saw... Can't we still be friends?'

When I answered, I was surprised at the lacklustre sound of my voice. 'You don't have to apologise to me,' I said airily. 'Sure, I've seen it all before.'

I remember the sadness in her eyes. My flippant remark probably told her more than just my words; it told her that her one-night stand had made me grow up all too quickly.

Later on – much, much later on – I realised that my youthful romantic imagination had created a perfect, illusive, godlike creature.

No matter how much
The saints to us
Preach and pray
Most people we love
And respect are born
With feet of clay.

CHAPTER 5

The Dublin Navvy

The social structures in existence when I was serving my time were rigid, dating as they did from the establishment of the Trade Guilds in the late seventeenth century. Then, there were basically only two types of people in these islands – those who were born to be attended to, and those poor unfortunates who had to attend on them. Even within the servants' quarters, a hierarchical system prevailed, and was jealously guarded by those at the top, such as housekeepers, butlers, head gardeners and such-like. This was considered a good, workable solution, as it encouraged those young people at the bottom to aspire to a better position within their own class structure.

So, when the factories and mills were in their infancy, the owners adopted this same kind of hierarchy: the manager passed on his instructions to the foreman, who in turn passed them on to the charge-hands. These were men who had been workers themselves, and who knew the workers and their capabilities; but, because of their lowly position, they often took a lot of stick off the foreman, and sometimes off the workers as well. This encouraged most of the charge-hands to become foremen, thereby carrying on the antiquated system. This same system of tuppence looking down its nose at a penny was, with slight variations, strictly observed by the guild members of the Western world. When a member had served his full apprenticeship and became a proper journeyman in his own right, he automatically assumed the title of 'Master' – notwithstanding the fact that the same journeyman might not even have an arse in his trousers.

In my youth, most of the old bricklayers and stonemasons were what my father would call 'oul' consequences, full of their own importance'. In my grandfather's time (at the turn of the century and right up to the early 20s) the bricklayers and other tradesmen had certain pubs that they and they alone frequented – and Lord help the non-tradesman who ventured inside and tried to rub shoulders with them, especially if the poor man happened to be a labourer! This was the term that was in common use even in my time, but unfortunately it had a derisive tone when used by a tradesman of that period.

I have tried, over the years, to rationalise this strange behaviour on the part of most tradesmen. The two building groups, trades and non-trades, were interdependent on each other; and furthermore, by the very nature of their work, the non-trades builders of that period were very knowledgeable in various aspects of building work – the laying of sewerage pipes, for example. Also, many were expert at scaffolding, one of the most responsible and highly skilled jobs in the whole of the building industry, and one on which the tradesman's very life depended.

Notwithstanding all this, the demarcation lines were firmly drawn, especially in the modes of dress. Whereas the tradesman wore a collar and tie with his bib-and-brace overalls, with the customary measuring rule projecting from his side pocket, the labourer wore a collarless shirt, a muffler and moleskin trousers, in which he always carried his sweat-rag and the price of two pints of plain porter.

As he drank these two pints, before mounting his bicycle and heading for home and a houseful of kids, the labourer was – often unknown to himself – participating in a ritual that was as old as the porter itself. This ritual started as soon as he left the building site and entered his pub. Heading straight for the bar, he'd wait to catch the barman's eye; having done so, he would simply nod at him, as one would on meeting an acquaintance in the street, then stand impassively until the first pint of plain porter was placed in front of him. Firmly taking hold of the glass, he'd hold it to his open lips – not sipping or gulping, but gently allowing nearly half of its nectar contents to pass through to his gullet before slowly removing the half-empty glass and placing it on the counter before him, while at the same time shoving out his tongue to clean the surplus froth from his unshaven face. Only then would he open his coat and produce a cigarette, usually a Woodbine or a Kerry Blue.

As soon as the last of its smoke became part of the foul-smelling air swirling around him, a benevolent smile would appear on his rugged face. Taking up the half-filled glass, he'd empty the rest of its contents down his throat, again using his tongue to ensure that not a drop was lost in transit. Then, catching the barman's eye again, he'd put his hand into the pocket of his moleskin trousers and slowly pull out the price of two pints of plain. The barman would place another large pint of porter in front of him and then, without saying a word, would scoop up the loose money and walk away, while the man himself lit another cigarette and looked up intently at the ceiling for a while as if he were a prospective buyer. After ten minutes or more of intense scrutiny, he would return his gaze to the matter at hand: taking up his pint glass, he'd place it to his lips and drink until not so much as a cold breath was left inside. He'd pass the back of his hand across his mouth and wipe it on the leg of his trousers; then, nodding to the barman, he'd turn and leave as quietly as he had come. After a short period, the barman would collect the empty pint glass from the counter and place it in a basin of water for its first wash of the night.

These men, living as they did on the borderline of poverty, due to large families and small wages (when they were lucky enough to secure any employment), reacted to their inferior situation in many different ways, some sad, some very funny. I remember one great character I worked with. He didn't drink much, but he was a great gambler – great, that is, from the bookies' point of view – and so he was known as Horsey. As he used to say himself: 'I back horses that should come in at 10 to 1, but they always seem to only come in at bleedin' tea-time.' Horsey was always keen to let you know that he led a full and interesting social life; one day he came in all excited, and told us that the night before he had been appointed the president of the Indian Betterment Society.

'What's that?' asked the Ganger (the foreman in charge of the labourers), winking at me.

'It's a society to create better relations between us and all them Indian fellas,' said Horsey without batting an eye. Then he added, 'When they handed me my chain of office, the whole group stood and clapped me.'

'And what did you do?' asked the Ganger.

'What could I do only bow,' said Horsey, showing us the way he'd returned the bow.

'I hope you weren't wearin' them trousers when you were takin' your bow,' muttered the old Ganger.

'Why not? What's wrong with them?' inquired the new President of the Indian Betterment Society.

'Oh, nothing,' said the Ganger. 'Only your dirty bare arse doesn't look too pleased at being exposed to all that there racial integration.'

In those far-off days, upstairs walls, which nowadays are always studded with hardboard, were built with concrete or breeze-blocks. I remember building a two-inch breeze-block wall at the top of a staircase, separating the toilet from the landing. As it was Saturday and we were only working a half-day, we were all packed and ready to go ten minutes before the whistle blew – all, that is, except Horsey. He had thrown his coat on the toilet pan that morning and had forgotten about it, and of course my fresh wall, now four and a half feet high, hid the coat. With time ticking away, he was getting panicky; as he kept saying, 'If that bleedin' whistle goes, I'll be lookin' for me coat in me own time.'

Just as the whistle's beautiful note echoed over the building site, Horsey remembered where he had left his coat – but in reaching over to retrieve it, he pulled a portion of my wall with him. As it followed him down the stairs, the foreman, who happened to be nearby, shouted, 'What's that noise?'

'I think it's thunder, sir,' said Horsey as he ran past the foreman for the bus, trying to protect his dignity and his bare arse with his mortar-covered coat.

One of the many indignities men had to suffer on many building sites in those days was the complete lack of proper toilet facilities. It was said that a bricklayer was the only tradesman who could and did pee against his own work, but it could be very embarrassing if one felt the need to let one's bowels move – and this did happen, especially on a Monday morning after a weekend of hard drinking. You'd see tradesmen jumping down from the scaffolding, their newspapers clutched in their large fists as they tried to outpace nature and all its consequences – for the washing-up facilities were also non-existent.

I was on a large building site out in Finglas in the early 50s, and our mate – a huge man who could, and did, carry a loaded hod as easily as a farmer carries a placard at a demonstration – suddenly took ill and had to be rushed to the hospital. Later we heard he was suffering from chronic constipation. A few days later I went to visit him in hospital. 'How are you?' I asked.

'OK,' said he. 'They got my bowels to move this morning.'

Just then the doctor came in. 'Are you related to this fellow?' he asked.

'No, Doctor, I work with him.'

He gave me a long, hard look. 'Will you do me a favour?'

'Certainly, Doctor. What do you want me to do?'

'Will you tell those lads on the building site to use proper toilet paper, not them bloody cement bags, or you'll all end up like your friend here!'

There were tears in his eyes with constipation,
He thought that he'd never go no more.
He was in such pain and desperation
That he would – if he could – destroy the floor.
The poor doctor sighed,
And then he cried,
'I don't know what I'm going to do at all!
Will you cut out this caper
And use proper paper,
And leave the cement-bags to joint the bloody wall!'

CHAPTER 6

Building Boom

'The foreman told me I have to report to Crampton's site in Ballyfermot first thing in the morning.'

My dad, my brothers, Johnny and Brendan, and my three sisters, Annie, Margaret and young Elizabeth, were sitting around the table at evening time, enjoying the tasty stew that our mother had just dished up, when I announced my news. It was the spring of 1948.

'Where in the name of Christ is bloody Ballyfermot?' young Brendan asked loudly. Our mother, passing his chair, neatly clipped his ear. 'We'll have less of that corner-boy talk in this house,' she said as she headed for the kitchen to make the tea. One learned never, ever to curse in our mother's presence.

In those days, before the distraction of television, our house was what you would call a 'talking' house, in which most of the happenings of the day were mulled over and discussed; and, of course, having four bricklayers in the family tended to tip the conversation in the direction of the construction industry. Even when I was a child, I remember my father – who always had a large selection of loose bricks stacked out in the back yard – showing us the many different bonds; if we showed any hesitation, he'd say, 'Remember, it's only a brick; it can't and it won't bite you.'

'Ballyfermot.' As he repeated the name, Da had a wistful,

almost sad look on his usually cheerful face. 'When you get a chance, son, look for an old graveyard.' Then he lapsed into silence, while we, being young, spoke and laughed about youthful things. It was several years before I found out what he meant.

Very early the next morning, I mounted my bicycle and headed for Ballyfermot, which, I had been told, lay far beyond the borders of Inchicore and civilisation. Arriving, I found fields that extended all the way to Lucan and beyond. I reported to the general foreman, a Mr Hanratty, and was told the conditions of work. The rules were few and simple: hours of work, 8.30am to 5.30pm; half an hour for lunch; and no, repeat, *no* ten o'clock tea.

'What year are you on?' asked the general foreman.

'Fifth year, sir,' I answered, hoping and praying he would not suggest a test to see what I was capable of doing. I suppose every age will always carry its own worries and fears, and I remember quite clearly being terrified in case I was given some job of bricklaying that I could not carry out.

The foreman looked me up and down like an old stonemason carrying out a examination on a piece of fine stone, not seeing its strength but looking for its flaws. After what seemed a lifetime, he slowly removed his unlit pipe from the corner of his mouth and, turning to Mr Carberry, the housing foreman, said, 'Put him on rising walls and we'll see how he shapes up.' I breathed a huge sigh of relief; for both these men were among the most respected foremen in the building industry at that time.

The job of rising walls, which I had been given, consisted of going into a house whose superstructure, or outer wall, was already in place and laying out and forming the interior walls from beneath the damp-course, often at a depth of three feet or more. Once you were given the layout sketch and measurements, it was a straightforward job.

My time in Crampton's was a fruitful and happy one. I acquired a lot of experience in various areas, including the bedding of granite steps and spud-stones (the two stones at the base of a hall door), the formation of arches and the laying out of squint blocks, which consisted of three brick houses in one. In those days, plasterers had to trowel paths, and bricklayers were expected to be able to lay out house drains, then gasket and seal the pipe joints with sand and cement for a water inspection by the Clerk of Works. This I did under the direction of an old bricklayer by the name of Mr Murphy, a wonderful teacher. May God rest him and all those other great tradesmen who helped me become a bricklayer. Some did it with a curse, others did it with a smile; to all of them I now say, rather belatedly but nonetheless sincerely, thank you, wherever you are.

Eventually I finished my time in Crampton's and became a journeyman. Being a full-fledged brickie entitled me to tool money and an hour's travelling time, which in those days was based on the distance from Nelson's Pillar to the site where you worked. With a full week and the extras thrown in, I received the sum of nine pounds, one shilling and sixpence – a good wage for that time, but still very hard-earned money.

I also made a lot of firm friends and met many real live characters, some funny and some just plain mad, who helped to make me the person I am today. There was one bricklayer known as 'the Solicitor' because, without any soliciting from you or anyone else, he would give you his advice – which was usually way over the top. One day he came up to me as I softened up the mortar on my board. 'Always keep your mortar moist by keeping a can of water beside the mortar-board,' he muttered. Then he added, 'Of course, that's only in the summer; in winter you won't have to bother.'

'Why not?' said I innocently.

'Because, sonny boy, in wintertime, when that east wind is

blowing and you're working high up on a gable, the mortar will always remain moist due to the constant drip from your bloody nose.'

Another time I commented on how cold and wet the morning was. The Solicitor put his hand on my shoulder. 'Sonny boy,' he whispered, 'never condemn the weather. When you waken always say, "This could be the last day of my life." And I guarantee one day your wish will come true.' Then, having imparted this unrequested piece of useless knowledge, he'd disappear, not to re-materialise until the whistle went.

Building sites are strange places to work. Although there are lots of men working with you, there are very, very few with whom you would become pals, or even friendly enough to discuss anything other than sport – and, as I was never interested in sport, I tended to be a bit of a loner. To me, friendship, real friendship, is about the meeting of minds – so I was delighted to find one such friend in Crampton's.

His name was Ollie Byrne, and he had won several boxing titles and championships long before I met him. I immediately sensed a kindred spirit in this tall, well-built fellow. We very soon discovered we had the same mindset, the same interest in reading, similar outlooks on life and, even more importantly, the same sense of humour.

As I mentioned, there was no tea allowed at ten o'clock – officially, that is; but Ollie and I were always devising new methods to ensure that we got our brew. I remember one drizzly day we had our billy-can on a makeshift fire that we had made by putting two concrete blocks on their edges, about eighteen inches apart, then placing about four bars – used as reinforcers for concrete – on top of the blocks to act as a grid. Although we were surrounded by stacks of concrete blocks, we were both huddled over the fire to try and prevent the smoke from spiralling upwards. So intent were we on our quest for the forbidden tea that we did not hear one of the junior foremen until he was almost upon us.

'What's going on here?' he inquired loudly. It was obvious he was enjoying his new authority.

Was I delighted that Ollie had trained as a boxer! No sooner had the foreman uttered his first word than Ollie snatched the hot can and held it behind his back with both hands. The speed of his hands had to be seen to be believed. Fortunately for us, the foreman was blinded by his own authority; he repeated his question, only this time he shouted even louder. 'I said, what's going on here?'

'Well, sir,' I stammered, 'you know how the firm is always telling us to keep the site tidy... Well – well, I thought it would be a good idea if I collected most of the old papers lying around and burned them.'

The foreman was an English ex-army man, wise in the ways of hygiene and little else, and he actually believed me – which made me wonder if we ever check who we give guns to! Turning to poor Ollie, who was standing there with his hands blistering from holding the hot can, he barked, 'Don't just stand there with your hands behind your back, man! Help this lad gather the rest of the papers.' Then, eyeing me, he asked, 'What did you say your name was?'

'Jones, sir,' I replied.

'And what's your name?'

'Jones, sir,' Ollie said, then added, 'We're brothers.'

As the foreman turned away, he muttered, 'Strange, very strange, the way brothers can differ...'

Our reason for giving him a false name was that there were so many men on the site that he could not remember everyone by name; besides, he was noted for his bad memory. Whenever he caught any of us doing wrong, we always said our name was Jones; him being English, and Jones being such a common English name, he was sure to forget us. As Ollie and I sat having our tea, we couldn't stop laughing as we pictured the poor oul' sod trying to tell the general foreman about the Jones brothers and how different they were.

Only once, in all the time I knew and worked with Ollie, did I see the side of him that his opponents in the ring feared – and, unfortunately, I happened to be the main cause of him getting into such a foul temper. It happened very simply, with no planning at all, as these things do.

The way I see it, it all started because the summer of '48 was such a glorious, long, hot summer. Ollie, working out in the open, would leave his bottle of milk and home-baked cakes in a cool corner of one of the many new houses under construction. According to him, his mother was renowned for her home baking, and nearly every day our Ollie would bring in a big selection of these small but mouth-watering cakes.

This particular morning, another young brickie and I were building rising walls when Ollie walked in and left his cakes and bottle of milk in the coolness of the opening that formed the fireplace. Saying, 'Keep an eye on them,' he went back outside to his exacting job of forming and pre-casting window-sills. The other brickie and I worked away in a silence that was only broken when Paddy, our mate, carried in a block or a bucket of muck and complained about the terrible heat outside. After about an hour of listening to him moaning about having to carry in blocks and mortar, and about what a thirst he had, I said to him in a low voice, 'If you're that bloody thirsty, put your mouth to that bottle of milk in the fireplace there.' There was always a bit of a devil in me!

Well, the mere mention of drink – even though it was only milk – seemed to make him float over to the fireplace with all the speed of a six-year-old on Christmas morning. Putting the bottle to his mouth, he drank and drank until I declare to God I swear I could see his tongue, as long as a giraffe's in the zoo, licking the bottom of the bottle. After putting it down, he stood over me like some guardian angel. 'Billy,' he said, 'that was a life-saver – a bloody life-saver. I'm sorry I didn't leave yeh much.' It was on the tip of my tongue to ask him whether he had at least removed his own tongue from the bottle; but then I thought, why spoil a lovely moment?

For the next ten minutes or so, Paddy was so in love with life that he actually tried to whistle; but, finding it rather dry on the lips, he soon began to complain again about the bloody heat. 'You might find another drop of milk in that bottle,' I whispered to him.

He looked at me strangely. 'Why are yeh whispering, Billy?' he asked.

'Oh, it's your man,' I said, indicating the other brickie with my thumb; he went along with the charade, pretending not to hear what Paddy and I were saying. 'He never buys milk, but he's always looking for mine. I'd rather see you drink it than him.'

As Paddy raised the empty bottle to his parched lips, I decided to go for broke. 'There's a couple of wee cakes there as well; you can have one,' I whispered. As Paddy grabbed the cake and went out the door, the other brickie came hurrying over to me. 'What's got into you, Billy? You know Ollie will go spare when he finds his milk and one of his mammy's cakes missing!'

The same thought had crossed my mind, but I could not find a satisfactory explanation, due to the terrible raw fear in the pit of my stomach – and it wasn't helped by Paddy coming in and again trying to whistle as he put down another block at my feet. He winked at me and muttered under his breath, 'Did your mother bake them cakes, Billy?' I nodded. 'Well, tell her from me she's a darling girlie with a bit of flour.'

Coming from Paddy, this was praise indeed, and I felt I had to respond with equal magnanimity. 'Seeing that you like them that much, Paddy, you can have the rest of them,' I said, completely convinced that the devil himself was speaking through my mouth. When I explained this to Ollie, years later, his only reply was, 'It wasn't the devil, Billy French. It was you speaking through your bloody arse as usual.'

After what seemed a very short while, Ollie came in and went over to the fireplace. It was then all hell broke loose. I saw him turning and coming towards me; bending down, he half-lifted me out of the cutting, shouting into my face, 'Where's my cakes and my milk? Tell me or I'll shake the shaggin' life out of yeh!'

It was at that moment I *knew* I was possessed by the devil, for who else would put such an un-heavenly and wonderful half-lie into my mouth? 'Ollie,' I half-screamed, 'I swear to Almighty God himself, I never touched your milk and cakes!'

I don't know why, but by some miracle Ollie believed me enough to release me. But, as I was sinking back into the comparative security of the cutting, who should walk in but Paddy, a well-fed look on his face. Sizing up the situation in a flash, he dropped the bucket of mortar and ran out the door as fast as his poor legs would carry him, with Ollie in hot pursuit.

Many, many years later, I was coming out of a church when I felt a hand on my shoulder. It was Paddy. Although older, he looked very well, and after introducing him to my wife Maeve I told him how well he looked. Then, without a by-your-leave, he launched into the saga of the milk and cakes. 'Your husband nearly got me killed, missus,' he said. 'And now he has the nerve to say I look well. A cur, missus, that's what you married – a real live cur.'

Then, fixing his new cap on the Kildare side of his head, he marched off, leaving me to face the hostile glances of the people nearby, including my own wife.

CHAPTER 7

The Road of the Child

Dublin lies in a basin; therefore her suburbs rise upwards, especially in the west of the city, where the rise, although gentle, is rather dramatic, especially from Islandbridge. When we were building the Ballyfermot housing estate – or 'scheme', as it was called in 1948 – the benchmark located at the Ranch (the part of Inchicore that joins it to Ballyfermot) was on a level with the top of Nelson's Pillar in the centre of Dublin city. I mention this fact to show that, although Ballyfermot is only about four miles from the Liberties, in my father's time those four short miles must have appeared, to those who travelled them in sorrow, to compare with the long road that Jesus took to Calvary.

When I first started to work in that vast housing estate of Ballyfermot, my father had asked me to locate an old graveyard; but I, being young, was only concerned with the living. But in the year of '52, when I was newly married and working as a fully fledged journeyman for a builder in Finglas, he told me he was sending me to Ballyfermot to work on the new brick houses that were being built on an extension of the old Killeen Road (now called Le Fanu Road). On my first day on the new site, an old painter said to me, 'Have you seen that old graveyard across in the lane there? It gives me the creeps, even in daytime.'

'Don't say you believe in ghosts,' I said, laughing.

'That's typical of you young fellows,' he answered. 'But let me tell you, when you're as old as me you'll believe in supernatural things. And I'll tell you something for nothing: there's many a troubled spirit lying over there in that old graveyard.'

His words intrigued me so much that I decided I'd go and see for myself. Later, during my lunch hour, I crossed the old Killeen Road and, having walked up a narrow lane, found myself in a small, overgrown burial-ground. This, I thought, must surely be the old graveyard that my father had told me about. It was completely overgrown; here and there headstones, twisted with age and neglect, had blended in and become part of the natural decay that covered the whole area. Even though there were men laughing and talking a few hundred yards away, I felt that same air of desolation and eeriness about the place that the painter had said he had experienced, and I was glad to leave its coldness for the sunshine outside.

That evening I dropped in on my mother and dad for a cup of tea on my way home. When I casually mentioned that I had found the old graveyard, my father asked, 'Wasn't it up a long lane?'

'Yes,' I replied. 'Do you know it? Have you been there?'

'Aye,' he said. 'Many, many years ago, when I was a lad. Things were very different then.'

I laughed. 'You mean the good oul' days, Da?'

'No, son,' he said, and there was a sadness in his eyes, as if he was remembering a more disturbing time. 'There was nothing that good about the "good oul' days", as they're called, and you tellin' me about that old, old graveyard brings it all back to me.'

'Brings back what?' my mother inquired, her eyes on him.

The Da's answer was to reach for and light a cigarette. Then, quietly sitting down in his favourite chair near the fire

– so that he could blow the cigarette smoke up the chimney – he told me the story.

'When I was a young fella, about thirteen years of age, the 1913 strike was on. As it lasted for about nine long months, there was terrible poverty in the city of Dublin – so much so that the dockers of Liverpool, showing great solidarity with their Dublin brothers, offered to take the starving children, of whom I was one, to England to feed and clothe them.'

'Is that true, Dad?' I asked, finding it hard to believe.

'Very true, son; but, unfortunately, it didn't happen. You see, the clergy preached that we poor hungry children shouldn't be exposed to the pagan ways of those English workers and their families.'

'What happened?'

'Well, as we were being marched down the docks, the priests with their tall hats and their holy-joe followers came out singing hymns – "Faith of Our Fathers" was one, I remember – and they drove us back home like cattle, to the safety of our tenements and that helpless look in the eyes of our parents, especially our poor mothers.'

As Da lapsed into silence, I ventured to ask what all this had to do with an old graveyard in Ballyfermot.

'Don't you see, son, somehow it's all connected,' he said. 'It's like some huge jigsaw that someone not of this world put together; and, because I'm now a man, I've lived to see some of the bits form a pattern – not the whole picture, mind you, but some bits of it.'

Visibly upset, he drew on his cigarette. When he had exhaled the smoke, directing it up the chimney, he spoke in a soft voice. 'Did you know that during that period, from the turn of the century up to the 20s, we in Dublin had the highest mortality rate in Europe – worse than the Gorbals in Scotland – and that two out of every five children died at birth in the slums of Dublin during that time?'

As my mother nodded in agreement, he continued, 'There wasn't a shilling to be earned – no social welfare or children's allowance like we have today, none of the other things people are entitled to in order to keep the wolf from the door and a bit of food in a child's belly. Terrible times, son, terrible times – and don't let them buckos cod you by telling you they were the good oul' days. Far from it. Anything but. Can you imagine an infant dying at birth because the poor mother was so undernourished she wasn't able to give birth to a healthy child? Then imagine, if you can, that you, as a father, are unable to give that child – your newborn son or daughter – a decent funeral, because you have no money for the burial.'

'So what would a man do?' I asked.

'What could he do, only bury the little angel illegally?'

'Illegally?'

'Yes. Some of the neighbours would go over to the nearby vegetable market and collect certain types of boxes and make little coffins. And, because drink was cheap, the local publican would give them half of a small barrel of ullage – the slops that overflowed into the sinks when publicans would be pulling a pint – for nothing.'

'And did you actually see this happen, Da – illegal burials?'

'I not only saw it happen, I was part of it. In the early hours of the morning, while it would be still dark, when all the drink had been drunk, the poor mothers would cry as the men loaded up the tiny little boxes – there was often more than one.'

He paused as if in prayer, then almost whispered, as if reliving a terrible nightmare, 'I remember on at least two occasions myself and my pal Jack Reynolds walked behind the horse and cart, with a fair sprinkling of men, as they drove out to a place called Ballyfermot – and there they would bury those poor little infants illegally.'

Even though we later worked together on several jobs, including Walkinstown Church, my father never spoke of this again. This way of keeping the horrors they had experienced – be it the terribleness of war or poverty – inside them was a part of the make-up of many men of his time. Such stories; such sadness.

Many years later, I told the story to a De La Salle Brother, who was also a local historian. He found it very interesting; many years ago, the road that ran alongside the old graveyard was known as Killeen Road, and he told me that all over Ireland there were Killeen Roads, for the word 'killeen', in the very old Irish language, meant 'road of the child'.

Today, that old burial ground has been incorporated by the Dublin Corporation into a large park. The only visible evidence of the troubled past is a large grass mound, on which the children of today happily play, unaware of the terrible tragedies buried beneath them.

CHAPTER 8

A Real Dublin Character

Over my years as a journeyman, I met many men; but, as is the nature of things, only certain people stayed in my mind. Even after all those years of moving from job to job and working with men on different types of brick, block, and even stonework, some faces remain fixed in my mind's vision – helped, no doubt, by some incident or other that, for some unexplainable reason, I can recall as if it had taken place only a short while ago, instead of over forty-five years in the past.

One such man was Ned the Bed, so called because, when asked how and where he had spent his weekend, he simply said, 'Bed.' Ned was a true-blue Dub: when asked if he was a labourer, he cried, 'I am not – I'm a hoxie.' This was a word used only in Dublin building circles, and it meant that this person was an all-rounder – that he could carry a hod, mix and lay concrete, attend brickies, painters, plasterers (or muck-spreaders, as we called them), roofers, plumbers and carpenters, lay sewer pipes, hang gates, set out and erect scaffolding, and so on. It took a very assured man or a bit of an eejit to lay claim to such a title, and Ned the Bed, I'm afraid, fell somewhere between the two categories.

I was working at the time for Paddy Wood, building houses in Sandymount. Paddy, although very strict, was a fair man who had a great working knowledge of building, and because of this vast knowledge he was not afraid to ask you for your opinion if a problem arose. This was very refreshing in the climate of the times: in the early 50s, most builders regarded the 'working man' as one who didn't work, while what we thought of most builders was at that time unprintable, due to the very strict censorship prevailing in Ireland right up to the 60s.

The number of men on the site was small, about twelve in all; but, because they were what was known as good handymen (meaning they could turn their hands to almost any type of job), there was a great closeness among them. There was big Pearse Bonner from Donegal, a handsome man in his late thirties, a fine mate and a very fast brickie. There was Mick Melody, a Mayo man who had spent many years in America on the trowel; when a problem arose you could always hear Mick singing, in a fine public-house voice, 'When Ireland lay broken and bleeding it called for the men of the West.' Also working with us was Paddy Whelan, a great Dublin character, who came from a long line of brickies; he was the same Paddy Whelan who had had the rather dubious honour of being interned in the Curragh camp with the famous writer Brendan Behan during the 40s. We brickies worked directly for George Erwin, a Mayo man, who got us work and paid us a few coppers over the accepted rate. I, being young and soon to become a father, felt honoured to be accepted by this tight-knit group.

And then there was Ned the Bed. The first sight I got of Ned is as clear in my mind as the morning it happened. This small middle-aged man came around the corner on a bike and crashed headlong into the large heap of sand that lay near the entrance to the site. As he unravelled himself from the bicycle, and from the shovel and lunch attached to it, I asked him if he was all right.

'Yes, why wouldn't I be?' he asked, slowly standing up, then staring at me intently before fixing his cap and dusting himself down.

'Because you've had a bit of an accident,' I stammered.

'That was no accident, mate. That was carefully thought out and planned,' said he with a sad smile that showed big gaps between his teeth.

'But you've just crashed into a heap of sand.'

'Aye, I know. It was the softest thing around. You see, I've no bloody brakes on the oul' bike.' Having untied his shovel and angled the cap on his head, he set off for the office as if this were an everyday occurrence.

Later, as we all sat having our ten o'clock tea, Ned inquired if there was a union rep on the job, stating that he was a paid-up member of Larkin's union. Big Joe Mansfield, who was sitting next to him, muttered that Barney collected the union money every Friday. 'Good,' said Ned. 'I love to keep me union card up to date.' He finished his tea and threw the dregs from the cracked cup into the fire, then removed a small cigarette butt from behind his ear, and lit it from the fire. 'This is me last butt. Is there a shop around here that sells fags?'

'Yes,' said Barney. 'I'll be going out later if you want some.' Ned the Bed looked quickly at Barney but said nothing. Then the talk turned to one of the lads who was out sick. 'Yes,' said Mick Fortune, 'he's out three weeks now. I think it's about time we made a bit of a collection for him.' As the regular heads around the fire nodded in agreement, Ned piped up, 'Why, what's wrong with him?'

'Well, he got a terrible wetting here about four weeks ago, and we thought it was a bit of a cold he got,' replied Joe. 'But the poor divil doesn't seem to be able to shake it off. I only hope it's nothing more serious, and him with a wife and four kiddies to feed. I bet he could do with a few bob.'

'How much do you usually give?' asked Ned the Bed, still sucking his butt.

'About a half-crown each,' answered Seamus, Paddy Wood's younger brother, who was the apprentice carpenter on the site at that time. He later went on to become a very successful builder in his own right, under the name of J.J. Wood. 'Well, put me down for a half-crown as well,' said Ned.

'No, you wouldn't be expected to give any money,' Joe said. 'You're only after starting here; besides, you don't even know Dick.'

'No, no, I insist – I don't like being an outsider. Who'll be collecting the few bob?'

'I will,' said Barney.

Ned the Bed drew deep on the dregs of the butt in his mouth; as the blue smoke poured down his nose, he looked hard and long at Barney. 'You're in everything but the Women's Sodality,' said he. 'And I bet you bloody well collect at the chapel door.'

Later, thinking about this man Ned, I marvelled at his individualism. Here we were, a tight-knit group, and within a few hours of arriving on the site he was being talked about – while he himself, with his sad unchanging face, seemed to think it was his duty to point out to us our many faults, reminding us that we had consciences.

Dublin was small at that time, and we belonged to a closed trade, so it was not unusual to meet the same brickies again and again, on different sites. This was inclined to create a complex situation; it was both a good and a bad thing. Working with other brickies you knew meant that you knew their capabilities, their weaknesses and their speed; if a brickie outpaced you on one job, next time you worked alongside him you felt honour-bound to outpace him. This meant you worked faster and laid more bricks – but, in doing so, you rushed yourself out of work that much quicker. Talk about killing the golden goose! But deep inside all of us, I suppose, there lies a competitive streak that drives us to be the fastest and the best; and so we found ourselves in daily competition with our fellow brickies.

A case in point was the time when Paddy Whelan and I were working for P.F. Fearon. Working permanently in that firm were two brothers from Dundalk by the names of Sammy and Chickie Houston. Chickie was a carpenter and Sammy was a brickie, and a very fine one he was, as neat as he was fast – and he was fast.

One day Paddy and I were detailed to form soldier arches, or 'flat' or 'camber' arches, as they are sometimes called, over some door and window openings. Because this type of arch depends on the key brick being wedged in, it called for some preparatory work on our part. Shortly after we started, who hops up on the scaffolding near us, ready to build identical arches, but Sammy, a low-sized figure who never removed his topcoat. Seeing that there were two of us, and that we had a head start, I whispered to Paddy, 'Let's give oul' Sammy a run for his money.' So, without even stopping for a smoke, we both got dug in, laying out and forming our two arches. But, as we were about to put in the key brick in the centre of the last arch, Paddy cried out, 'Christ, the oul' shagger is finished before us!' And, sure enough, there was oul' Sammy – and he old enough to be our father – standing there with a cigarette between his lips and just a hint of a smile on his weather-worn face.

The next time Paddy and I found ourselves working together, one of the houses we were building was for a builder by the name of McGuinness, a former bricklayer who in his youth had won a gold medal for bricklaying. Of course he kept a very close eye on our work, and we, being conscious of this, were delighted when he commented favourably on the brickwork and mentioned that the inside walls were as neat and tidy as he had seen in a long time.

Such comments merited a special response from us, and several days later Paddy Whelan told me what he had in mind. As we formed the walls that divide the flue-liners inside the chimney-stack, I heard Paddy ask one of the lads if he had anything that would make a flag. Knowing his background, I thought for a minute that he was going to declare a republic in Sandymount, but he soon informed me that he was going to resurrect an old building custom: by hoisting the flag, you informed the owner that his house was finally built. And, to give him his due, when Mr McGuinness saw the flag he immediately gave Paddy a twenty-pound note to treat everyone on site to a drink. This was big money, when you think that we were earning about eleven pounds a week and a pint of stout cost about two shillings and threepence.

Later that evening, Paddy, acting as box-man, ordered a round of drinks for everyone on the site – even for those who hadn't come, which meant we had to drink theirs as well. Then we stood with full glasses of stout and toasted Mr McGuinness. After toasting him about half a dozen times more, I decided to head home to Crumlin. As I rose to leave, Ned the Bed attempted to stand up but was somewhat hampered, not by the pints of stout, but by the whiskey chasers.

'Are – are you on – on a bike?' he muttered, pointing at me.

'Yes,' I said, peering at him. 'Why do you ask?'

'Be – because you're in no fi – fit state to ri – ride a bi – bicycle,' said he, grabbing my left leg the way a one-legged mountaineer would cling to the top of a glass mountain. He tried to rise from the floor, and I half-carried him outside. As I stood him against the wall, he started to cry.

'What's up with you, Ned?' I asked.

'Are – are you su – sure you're all right, Billy, go – going home on – on that bike?'

'Of course I'm all right. Can't you see I'm all right?'

'Well,' said he, sobbing gently, 'at any ti – time, Billy, you're not a pretty sight; and now, to my so – sorrow, I can se – see two of you.' He threw his leg over the saddle of his own bicycle and fell with a terrible thud on the other side.

Out of the darkness came two very large policemen. One grabbed Ned by the scruff of the neck while the other held the bike; then, placing him on the saddle, they pushed him into the darkness. Talk about ships in the night. We never saw Ned the Bed again.

CHAPTER 9

Marriage Discussed

From Paddy Wood's site I was sent by George Erwin into Warrenmount convent school, near New Street, to point up and repair old brickwork with sand and cement. There are certain bricklayers, called wiggers, who specialise in this type of work. I'm afraid that, on the Judgement Day, no matter what the Angel Gabriel calls me, it won't be 'wigger'. The work didn't suit my temperament – too much standing in one position, with a small pointing trowel in one hand and a small board (called a 'hawk') in the other hand.

Then there was the foreman. He was a simple man (with the emphasis on 'simple') with notions of grandeur. This was especially evident first thing in the morning, when he would appear at one of the windows on the top floor of the school; looking down at the four of us, he would give us the day's instructions – which were, in essence, more of the same. After his little speech he would disappear into the Twilight Zone, only to reappear at the same window in the evening. Opening the window slowly, he would study his watch with all the intensity of a blind referee on an ice rink before blowing his whistle very loudly. This wasn't necessary; as he was so predictable, the minute we saw him appear at the window, we would jump down off the scaffolding, grab our bikes and be out of earshot before the little pea even started its dance inside his lovely shiny whistle.

The day George Erwin informed me that I was being shifted out to Lady Shaw's old estate at Rathfarnham was a great relief for me. Working in a girls' secondary school, you couldn't express yourself in vulgar terminology as you would normally do if some eejit working with you were to stand on your toe. So, having hastily packed my tools and tied my large level onto the crossbar of my bicycle, I was ready for the road – that is, after the customary visit to the toilet.

There were three pans, one separated from the other two by a large sheeting board; this hidden toilet was reserved for the foreman. As the other two toilets stood side by side, I could not but notice that an old painter was sitting on one of them, his off-white trousers down around his ankles, smoking a small clay pipe. He seemed at peace. I, being in a happy mood due to the fact that I was moving to the new site in Rathfarnham, was singing rather loudly as I unzipped the front of my overalls and watched the waters flow. It was then that I heard the foreman's loud voice coming from the other side of the enclosed partition.

'Hey, you in there, whoever you are, stop that singing!'

I finished washing my hands and slowly edged nearer the partition until my mouth was almost touching it. Then I said loudly, 'Hey, you in there, whoever you are, would you ever go and shit yourself!'

Satisfied that somehow I had at least regained my manhood, I strolled towards the door – nearly falling over the poor oul' painter, who was swearing that he had always known I was a little bastard. As he was struggling with his braces, belt and trousers, I reminded him, as gently as I could, that he hadn't pulled the chain. I could still hear him raining down curses – not just on me, but on my poor mother and father as well – as I shook the dust of the city off myself, mounted my trusted old bicycle and headed for the hills; for Rathfarnham was (and still is) at the foot of the Dublin mountains.

I can't say I was introduced to the foreman brickie when I arrived on the site. Somebody pointed him out to me, and as I approached him, he in turn pointed to the scaffolding surrounding a half-built brick house. After indicating with his hand that I should join the other 'trowels' up there, he turned and was gone.

This was my first association with Dan McConnall. A Cavan man by birth, he was a tough but very fair man who taught me a great deal about bricklaying and other sections of the building game. His knowledge of building had been passed on to his three sons, Jimmy, Tommy and Danny, three very good brickies. They became great friends of mine, and because we were young we were up to all kinds of devilment.

For instance, the toilet arrangements were very, very basic: just a large trench about nine feet long, six feet wide and ten feet deep, surrounded by six-foot-high lengths of galvanised sheeting. If one wanted to discharge one's urine, one had to stand with one's back to the hoarding, on a grass path measuring less than eighteen inches wide; but if one had a bowel movement, one would want to do a very quick course as a contortionist in Duffy's Circus before attempting the almost impossible. Having dropped your trousers and underpants, you had to position yourself so that the large trench was behind you; no matter how tightly you tried to crouch down, the crown of your head invariably touched the nearby galvanised sheeting.

One day Jimmy and I, after cutting and trimming a large concrete head, were passing the 'toilet', and we couldn't help noticing this poor oul' brickie crouched down inside, for he had that constipated look of agony on his deeply lined face. We, both being good Catholic boys, decided that we would help him with his bowel movement. Positioning ourselves outside the galvanised sheeting, we raised our lump hammers and hit the sheeting with such force that we were sure it could only do good. But then, after a silence, an almighty roar came from inside that primitive urinal, telling us that our Christian act had backfired. So we did what any lads would do: we ran like hell. Later, the two of us were first in line to sympathise with the Sheik, as he was now being called due to the large bandage that completely covered the top of his head.

This type of toilet, if it can be so called, was in use on a lot of building sites at that time; and of course many a story relating to them was told, true and untrue. One of the oldest of these stories was the one where a man complained to the foreman that, while he was in the toilet, his jacket had fallen into the trench.

'What do you want me to do about it?' shouted the foreman. 'Do you want me to jump in after it?'

'Oh, no, sir,' the man replied. 'As a matter of fact, the oul' jacket is past its best; but you see, sir, me lunch is in the inside pocket.'

These were the primitive conditions the building workers had to endure up to the 50s and beyond. We were out in all weathers, existing all day on tea and sandwiches – which had probably been cut and buttered the previous night – then, after a hard day's work, cycling home against wind and rain. On some jobs the builder would erect a hut – not for us, but for the bags of cement that were being used on the site. So in most cases, you placed your lunch, wrapped in last night's *Herald* or *Evening Mail*, in the hut, on a plank of wood that was raised nine inches off the ground by two old concrete blocks, so that rats, mice or other vermin couldn't reach it.

I remember once I heard the whistle blow and came down off the scaffolding, only to discover that my lunch – or what was left of it – was scattered on the ground. Someone said they had seen an old greyhound sniffing around earlier. Just then, the same old greyhound came limping up to a tall, grey-haired painter – his name was John Little, so of course we called him Little John – who offered it some bread. I couldn't understand this, for his lunch had also been destroyed. My blood was at boiling point: because of this mangy-looking dog, I was going to have to do without food until I got home at around seven o'clock that evening. The hunger pangs already tearing at my empty stomach demanded retribution. Grabbing an old stick, I advanced on the miserable-looking bag of bones.

'Put down that stick.' The words, quietly spoken, made me pause.

'But he ate your lunch as well,' I stammered, my temper still rising. But Little John was adamant.

'Drop the stick,' he repeated. 'Is there no Christian feeling in your make-up?'

'What do you mean? He's after eating my bloody lunch!'

'Did you never ask why he ate it? It's because he's hungry too,' said Little John, still feeding the greyhound from the scraps of bread lying about. At the same time he rubbed the dog gently on his head, along his long narrow body, down to his tail and underneath. The old greyhound was standing very quietly; you could see he was really enjoying all this attention. Little John's hand travelled all the way down to the greyhound's private parts, gently rubbing, while he talked to him in a soothing voice that was almost lulling him to sleep.

But then, all of a sudden, as if struck by lightning, the greyhound leaped forward. Howling like a deranged wolf, he dashed away, upsetting and scattering cups of tea in all directions.

All eyes went to Little John, who by way of explanation held up his hand – the same hand with which he had been gently rubbing the greyhound's body and private parts. It revealed a small pad; and, even from a good distance, one could not help but inhale the strong smell of turpentine.

Dog lovers will probably be very upset about this story; but, as Little John said, 'It's a dog-eat-dog world, and he won't attempt to eat my bloody lunch again.'

Another day, as we sat having our lunch, the conversation turned to women in the workplace – how hard it was on them trying to get young children out to school, run a house, and hold down a job at the same time. As we sat back, drinking tea in the glorious sunshine, our hearts really went out to these poor overworked ladies – well, all our hearts but one: Little John was firmly against the idea of any woman working outside the home, and said so several times.

'But some women have to work, to help pay the rent and the bills,' explained Peter the roofer.

'It's the man's job to do the providing, and it's the woman's job to run the home. That's the way Nature intended.'

'But what if the man's money isn't enough to run the house – what then?' asked the brickie's mate (who was known as Veggie, because he had a cauliflower ear), as he lit his pipe and thought of his own wife holding down two cleaning jobs.

'Well, he should make sure he's the provider,' replied Little John. 'Otherwise he has no right to ask a girl to marry him.'

'But what happens if a man, through no fault of his, falls sick, or can't get a job? Isn't it better if his wife is working? It keeps the wolf from the door,' cried Peter.

'Wolf, me arse,' replied Little John. 'Any man worthy of his salt should provide for such things as sickness and unemployment.'

'How?' shouted Veggie, trying again to light his pipe.

'By giving up your smoking and your drinking,' whispered Little John, his voice dripping with malice. 'And your gallivantin' in your marriage bed.'

'Does your wife go out to work?' asked Veggie.

'She does not,' quickly answered Little John.

'And what does she do all day?' asked Veggie, well aware that Little John and his wife had no family.

'She gets my dinner!' shouted Little John. 'That's what she does – she gets my dinner!'

'By Jaysus, it must be some dinner she gives yeh, if she starts getting it ready at eight o'clock in the morning,' replied Veggie, as the whistle called us to return to work.

Next day, Nature, just to show us the uncertainty of the Irish weather, sent us down a fine shower of snow. As I scampered for cover against the gable of a house, who should be there but Veggie. Just then, around the corner came Little John, covered from head to toe with snow.

'By Jaysus, man,' said Veggie, removing his pipe from his mouth. 'You're goin' to get some dinner tonight.'

'What do you mean?' asked Little John.

'I was passing your house a while ago, and your wife was out pulling cabbage in the snow,' said Veggie, shoving his pipe back into his mouth, highly satisfied that he was after having the last word.

CHAPTER 10

McCarthy and the Embankment

Bricklayers in my time did not belong to a trade union; as I have mentioned, we belonged to a guild – the Ancient Guild of Incorporated Brick and Stonelayers. As we were a closed trade that had been established in the seventeenth century, we tended to have inside knowledge of fellow bricklayers' family trees; it was quite common to hear one old brickie, when talking about another, preface his remarks by saying, 'I knew all belonging to him, and none of them, no matter how far you go back, was ever any bloody good.'

One member of the Bricklayers' Hall (as we called it) who entered the history books was the infamous James Carey. A member of the 'Invincibles', he was involved in the Phoenix Park murders in May 1882, when Undersecretary T.H. Burke and the newly appointed Chief Secretary, Lord Frederick Cavendish, were killed. Carey's alleged confession, trial and subsequent death by shooting aboard ship off the coast of Australia are still remembered in song and story.

If ever you travel down to hell
And look in the farthest corner,
There you will see oul' Skin-the-goat
And Carey the informer...

Skin-the-goat was the jarvey-man who drove the group of Invincibles to and from the park on that terrible May morning in 1882. He was so called because it was said he always wrapped himself up in a goat's skin which stank to high heaven; he himself had taken the same skin off the poor goat and hadn't applied any curing measures, so you could smell him before you saw him or his horse. It could be just another folklore story!

What is not so well known is the fact that Carey, as well as being a bricklayer, was also a City Councillor, and that for his work in the City Council he was presented with an address in the form of a scroll in the Bricklayers' Hall, for the time and effort he put into preventing a Scottish firm of bricklayers from getting the contract to lay the main sewerage system in Dublin city, thereby creating more work for his fellow brickies.

Another name that made the history books was that of Richard O'Carroll, who was shot dead in the 1916 rebellion. At the time of his death he was the President of the Bricklayers' Guild. He was one of the Labour leaders on the Dublin City Council and an officer in the Citizen Army under James Connolly. He was captured in Camden Street and marched into a back yard where it is alleged he was shot by a Captain Colthurst – the same officer who, it is said, had shot the pacifist Sheehy-Skeffington earlier that day. At a court-martial held later, Captain Colthurst was found guilty but insane. One of my earliest recollections of the Bricklayers' Hall is of seeing a large painting or photograph of Richard O'Carroll in pride of place on the wall, and I'm sure at times I detected a cynical little smile on his face as he listened with the silent minority to the very heated debates that took place within those august walls.

For all tradesmen have gripes, but especially the poor bricklayers. We had to work under foremen who were, for the most part, carpenters, and these foremen's one aim was to get us off the site as quickly as possible so that, as they said themselves, 'the real work (i.e. putting on the roof) could be started'. This in itself caused conflict, and the only place where the bricklayer could air his grievance, imaginary or otherwise, was at the meetings in the Hall. And this is what the vast majority did – only they did it not individually but all together, each trying to shout the other voices down, which led to some very amusing moments.

At one very stormy meeting, the Secretary and acting Chairman was trying to bring a wee bit of not just order, but sanity, to the proceedings. He shouted, 'Silence, and give the Chairman a chance!' A sort of miniature silence prevailed, but it ended rather rudely when the acting Chairman, using his best parliamentary language, announced that 'the Chair recognised the speaker in the front row' – only to hear an old bricklayer at the back of the Hall shout, 'And why wouldn't you recognise him? Isn't he your own effin' brother!'

I remember, at one particular meeting, standing up to support the committee on some recommendation, only to be shot down by voices shouting, 'Lick-arse!' and other uncomplimentary remarks. This always amazed me. The committee was always voted in, by secret ballot, by the members themselves; but once installed, the committee was, due to some perverse thinking of the day, deemed to be the enemy, and their suggestions to the members were always attacked and thrown out. But I, being young, idealistic and full of fight, persisted in defending the legal right of the committee to direct us. I went even further and said it was their duty to recommend a certain course of action for the rank and file members to follow.

After some more catcalls and a lot of explicit language, a Kerryman's voice, formed and honed in the hills around Listowel, was heard from the back of the Hall calling for order and a chance to address the meeting. Such was the respect in which this man was held that the acting Chairman immediately acceded to his request.

'Mr Chairman,' he began, 'everyone, especially those that are married and trying to do the best for our wives and families, knows that we are not paid half enough for the time and the skill, fashioned over generations, that we give to building up this great country of ours. But if you were to listen to that diabolical proposal from the committee, in which they call for restraint, they would have you working for the same wages our poor grandfathers worked for, while the capitalist builders grow fatter by the day on our sweat, blood and knowledge.'

Of course, this kind of speech was sure to inflame the body of the Hall; old and young men clapped and shouted in agreement. After about three very noisy minutes, the silver tones of the Kerryman again cut across the Hall as he implored the members not to be too hard on 'the last speaker' (meaning me) – 'because we all know he is Jesuitly orientated,' he explained. This was a veiled reference to the fact that I was a part-time student in Milltown Jesuit College; having left school at the tender age of thirteen and a half, I felt the need of education and had taken full advantage of the classes being run there under the keen guidance of Father Kent SJ.

This Kerryman was a bricklayer by the name of Mick McCarthy, who always said that he was 'a converted Socialist but a born Republican'. He and I had many an argument on the floor of the Hall, but later we both served on the same committee, and a very real and lasting friendship sprang up between us. Although our views were diametrically opposed, I soon found that he was a very caring man, especially where old people were concerned. He organised concerts, in the Hall and elsewhere, for old and retired bricklayers and their families. These concerts were sell-outs; the artists appearing were all top-class acts, and they gave their time and talents free of charge because of 'Uncle Mick', as he was affectionately called by his friends. Such was the measure of the man that the real Dublin brickies accepted him as one of their own – and this was in the time of Brendan Behan, who used to say that he was brought up in a Dublin where anything that moved beyond Inchicore was either a cow or a culchie!

Incidentally, Brendan – who was a well-known writer even then – was a very close friend of Mick McCarthy's, as were Paddy Whelan, Cathal Goulding and other well-known Republicans. When one got to know Mick, as I was privileged to do, one soon learned that, deep down, he had a very real, almost childlike passion for the old Celtic Ireland that had borne him. He loved its stories, its music, its songs and dance; he once told me that he felt he was truly 'one of the rocks of Bawn'. To be in his company with a drink before you, a pipe in your mouth and the darkness of the night outside, and he telling stories of a Kerry that has all but faded into the mists of time, was a tonic that could and did only benefit the listener. As one was transported back to the terrible poverty brought about by civil war, and the innocence of the womenfolk who believed it was all 'the will of God', one could almost hear the music from the streams as Mick and his brother Sean fished for salmon while another brother kept a sharp lookout for the bailiffs – for it would surely be the jail for any Irish boy caught bagging a salmon from an Irish stream; every Irish boy was supposed to know that all the fishing rights in Ireland belonged to the absentee landlords, and that Irish people should never try to claim equality with their 'betters'. These were the times that had spawned Mick McCarthy and his generation.

'When I was a lad,' Mick would say, his dark eyes full of mutiny, 'there was a cousin of mine and a namesake doin' the jail for catching a small thraneen of a salmon that could have easily passed for a grown-up sardine.' Then a note of devilment would creep into his voice. 'Even the priest in the confession box would go easy on the poor sinner the minute the word "poaching" was whispered in his ear; he'd bloody nearly give you the Pope's blessing with the absolution – whereas if you told him you'd put your hand up a girl's dress, he'd nearly read your name off the altar the followin' Sunday.'

Mick's eyes would cloud over. 'Strange, the power of the salmon,' he'd say, as his mind wandered back to that Kerry of his youth. 'You know, it played a big part in Greek mythology...' And he'd launch into a song that was as long as it was broad.

One day he went up to build a large granite fireplace in a small pub, just outside the town of Tallaght, called the Embankment. It was a name that would become synonymous with the Irish ballad and would be forever associated with Mick McCarthy – for the upshot of it was that Mick ended up buying the small pub. He immediately set about building on large extensions (I myself laid out one of them) to cater for the vast crowds that flocked out to the 'Bank every evening, especially at weekends to hear such groups as The Dubliners, The Wolfe Tones, The Fureys, Johnny McEvoy and Patsy Watchorn, as well as the resident Saturday-night group, Platform. As I sat and listened to Ray Kennedy's silver tones singing about the cliffs of Dooneen, Billy Merriman's guitar-playing or the complementary sound of the banjo played by Brian O'Connor, how could I have imagined that many years later my own son-in-law, Martin Corcoran, would be a part of that very versatile group as they played for the Americans and other tourists, telling them through song and story that 'only our rivers run free'?

The foreword of Mick McCarthy's book *Early Days* was written by that great Irish writer Bryan MacMahon, who had taught Mick in the Listowel national school many years before. In it, Bryan – who, incidentally, had also been a teacher in my own school, Scoil Treasa Naofa – tells a lovely story of going up to the Embankment one Saturday night. As he was fighting his way in, he was confronted by a man 'whose eyes were filled by merriment and mutiny.' As recognition dawned, the man gripped Bryan and dragged him bodily up onto the stage. Those present looked up in amazement. 'Shut up, you so-and sos,' Mick McCarthy shouted. 'When I was a barefooted boy in Kerry, I had a dream that I'd own a joint as big as this, and that Master MacMahon would come and visit me. Here he is now – and, by God, the so-and-so house is his.' Bryan MacMahon's foreword then goes on to say that a schoolmaster builds neither bridges nor houses; he has nothing to show for his time except memories – like the memory of that night in the Embankment, which he treasured. It was fitting that he should finish his foreword in pure Kerry style: 'Be off with you, Mick, it's been a long day. But school at last is over.'

During the 70s, many well-known artists, including Mícheál Mac Liammóir and Josef Locke, appeared on the stage of the 'Bank. But notwithstanding these and other illuminating names, one of the main reasons people returned to the 'Bank time and time again was Uncle Mick himself. He was such a popular figure that he was voted Lord Mayor of Tallaght for his charity work, and for this great occasion I put pen to paper and came up with the following verse.

There was a man, a mighty man,
Good-natured, kind and hearty,
Who became the Mayor of Tallaght town,
By the name of Mick McCarthy.
Although he was poor, this Kerry hoor
Carried a bricklayer's trowel
With his two brown boots and shiny suit

When he left his own Listowel.
With other Micks he laid the bricks
In London's diminishing tillage,
Then came back home, no more to roam,
To lovely Tallaght Village.
He built a pub, a mighty pub,
On the road to Blessingtown,
With The Dubliners, The Platforms, The Fureys
And other bands of great renown.
The people of Tallaght adopted him
For the great work that he did
For the aged, the poor and the lonely,
When a quid was worth a quid.
For they knew they were always welcome
In his pub of cobweb threads,
So they dressed him in robes down to his toes
And a hat they placed on his head.
They seemed to come from everywhere
To hear words of wisdom from his lips.
Some died laughing at his jokes,
While others choked on his chicken and chips.
Then they placed a chain around his neck
That nearly reached the ground,
And in saying the prayer, he was made aware
He was now the Mayor of Tallaght town.

It was said by some people (but not by me) that no one ever saw a pigeon flying within three miles of the 'Bank – for it was said (but, again, not by me) that any pigeon that did could end up in the next batch of chicken and chips. It was also said (again, not by me) that for pigeons the blue skies over the Embankment were a sort of Bermuda Triangle.

My final word on Mick came in the late 70s, when there were a lot of Kerryman jokes doing the rounds of the building sites. I had a small book of poems launched at the Listowel Writers' Week, and I included the following verse, entitled 'McCarthy the Brickie from Kerry'.

Irish builders bred great men,
From Cork to the city of Derry,
But the best on the trowel
Was a man from Listowel,
McCarthy – the brickie from Kerry.
'I want a wall built quick,'
The builder cried,
'As high as you can go.'
Well, up jumped Mick with a load of bricks
And he laid them in a row.
He worked all day for little pay,
Bedding brick and stone,
Then home to bed with a pain in his head –
He awoke to the sound of the phone.
'It's the dead of night, you gave me a fright!
Who's that ringing, may I ask?'
'Is that you, Mick? You better come quick –
The bloody moon is wanting to pass.'
Mick got to the foot of the wall
And started to climb to the top,
Halfway up the ladder,
An astronaut told him to stop.
'Say, why did you build this damn wall so high?'
The Yank said with a grin.
'You upset our calculations, man,
We thought we were in Berlin.'
'No, this is Ireland, sir,' the brickie replied,
His eyes bright and merry.
'God damn it, man,' the astronaut cried,
'It's McCarthy the brickie from Kerry.

Say, why don't you build a pub up here?
You need never pay no rent.
And call it some fancy name –
Like the old Em-bank-ment.'
'Well, I thought of that, sir,' McCarthy replied,
But I'm knockin' this wall to rubble.
You see, the police is outside –
And I've nowhere to hide –
And I'm in diabolical trouble.'
So they led him away
From his famous wall
So as not to anger the Jerry,
To live out his dream
Near the old town of Sneem –
McCarthy the brickie from Kerry.

Men like Mick McCarthy made me proud to be a brickie. It was a meeting of two trowels.

CHAPTER 11

The Magic of Kerry

When I finished my time as an apprentice and became a journeyman, I was following in the footsteps of generations of tradesmen who, down through the centuries, had literally built up the country, stone upon stone, brick upon brick. When I take a trip to the south or west of Ireland, I don't look with awe at the waters of the Lee or the Corrib, for these are natural water-courses; I reserve my veneration and wonder for old buildings – and not just for churches and such like. I have often found myself standing in front of an old stone pier in the middle of nowhere, wondering what the brickie or stonemason was thinking as he laid and plumbed this or that stone so many, many years ago. Was he dreaming of home? Was he old, at the end of his days? Did he hear the Grim Reaper in the silence of the countryside that surrounded him? Or maybe he was young, full of vitality and thinking of the young girl in the farmhouse behind the hill... Standing in the very spot where he once stood, I try to form a mental picture of that particular craftsman. Giving wings to my imagination, I wonder what county he hailed from – maybe from Dublin, like myself; and maybe, just maybe, he was a distant relation of mine, bonded to me by brick and stone.

For to be a journeyman in the nineteenth century meant just that: that you journeyed for work. It was a time when wheelwrights, boot-makers, wiggers, thatchers, stonemasons and brickies travelled the four corners of Ireland, crossing and re-crossing the Liffey near Thomas Street, which became a watering-hole for all travellers. At one time that area had more alehouses and doss-houses than anywhere else in Dublin. And it was from there that the journeyman, after refreshing himself with women and drink, set forth once more on his travels, picking up and distributing pieces of useful and non-useful information and gossip, which were often conveyed to the eager listener in the form of song or verse, bringing to the fore his old Celtic heritage.

Even in my time, song and verse were always part and parcel of our childish games. In his book *The Green Fool*, Paddy Kavanagh tells the story of a man who knocked on his door one Sunday and inquired whether the poet lived within. When Kavanagh invited him in, the man told him he was living among the worst of neighbours and asked whether, if he supplied the facts and the names of the neighbours, Paddy would compose a couple of verses or even a good poisonous ballad about them.

'What would you charge me for such a ballad?' inquired the man.

'Three pounds,' said Paddy.

'Three pounds!' said your man. 'Sure, I'd be better off sending them a solicitor's letter. I thought you might do it for the price of a couple of bottles of porter.'

I tell the story to show that ballads and verse were still very much in use in the 30s as means of conveying news that had taken place, maybe in a nearby village. In those days elderly women, having no television to run home to, would often gossip and gossip when they met, until their voices went right through you. 'You gossip like an oul' woman,' was a common saying if you talked too much. Many men – especially journeymen, when they arrived at their port of call for the night – gossiped in verse.

There is a red-haired woman
Living in yonder glen
Who hates her fat oul' husband
But loves most other men.
Six fine healthy children
Sleep by her side.
Strange men come and go at night,
While the husband sleeps outside.

After hearing this snippet of a verse, the women of the house would spend the whole night trying to figure out who it was that lived in the glen, hated her husband and loved other men. Meanwhile, the man of the house and his old neighbours, smoking their clay pipes and sipping the real Irish brew, knew from experience who the lady was; so they remained silent, not wishing to draw attention to themselves – thus maintaining the reputation of the silent sex.

I remember being in the town of Listowel, in the Kingdom of County Kerry, a number of years back. I was there at the behest of a returned Yank who was having a bungalow built in the townland of Finogue, and he had asked me to give it the once-over to see that everything conformed to building regulations. Having arrived late in the evening and settled into my digs, I decided to go for a quiet drink in one of the many public houses in the town. No sooner had I ordered a drink and started looking around for a seat than I was approached by two men, one elderly and one younger.

'Good night, sir,' the young man said pleasantly. 'Weather's bad for this time of year.'

'Aye,' I replied, reaching into my pocket for my pipe.

'You're from Dublin, then?' the young man inquired.

I looked at him in amazement. 'Why do you say that?'

'By your accent, sir,' said he, gulping down his pint. As I watched him swill the last drop down his throat, I could not help reflecting on the fact that all I had uttered was the word 'aye'.

'You live around here?' It was my turn to have an inquiring mind.

'Aye,' said the older man, and I noticed that he hadn't a tooth in his head. 'Aye, man and boy. Born and reared in the rough times, sir. You were lucky to be born in Dublin.'

'How do you make that out?' said I, still not saying I was from Dublin.

'Well, you, being born in the Big Smoke, could pinch an apple from a fruit-stall if you were hungry, like, while the only things we could eat around here were the small stones in the field.'

I finished filling my pipe and, striking a match, watched it dance across the top of the bowl. 'What did they taste like, the stones?' A cloud of smoke followed my words into the already stale and cloudy air.

'Ah, all right, boy, but they sure played hell with your teeth,' said he, making a grim face, as if remembering what it was like to eat a stone.

How is it that older men are almost always obsessed with the hard times of their youth? And the more they drink, the poorer they were when they were young. All through my youthful days I heard how hard and how long these old-timers worked; and all I can say is, they must have worked these same characters to a stand-still, for I found that the majority of them wouldn't or couldn't work in a fit.

Then, as the drink flowed, I found myself telling these two total strangers how I myself often cycled ten miles to work only to find there was no work due to bad weather.

'You're at the building, then?' the younger man asked.

'Why do you say that?' I answered, being as cagey as he was, for I had been told to tell no one why I was there.

'Because you said about no work due to bad weather,' he

answered, winking at the older man.

'That doesn't mean I work at the building game,' I said, slurring my words as the drink took charge, delighted to think that I hadn't given any information to these two inquisitive Kerrymen. 'It could be any type of work. As a matter of fact, I could be a cricketer.'

'A cricketer? I don't follow yeh, boy.'

'It's easy: if I was a cricketer, living in this climate, rain would often stop play.' The laughter that followed was loud but genuine. 'Will you have another on us before we go?' the older man asked.

'No, thanks,' I said. 'I'd better be getting to my digs. Have you two far to go?'

'No, not too far,' the older man said. 'Sure, we're livin' only a stone's throw from that bungalow you're goin' to look at tomorrow. Safe home, now.'

I tell that true story to show how cautious and how shrewd the Kerryman really is. He's like an old grandfather clock, benign, gentle and gracious, his deep melodic tones ready to pour forth on any subject, making him a very enjoyable companion – and meanwhile you feel that, inside, his brain is working overtime to outwit and outsmart you. Coupled with these attributes is an innate love of the old-time culture that dates back to the dawn of history. One feels this timelessness as one travels Kerry's mountains or speaks to its people in their isolation amid the hills.

In my travels as a journeyman I was privileged to meet many a Kerryman; and in my search for culture I was fortunate enough to rub shoulders with writers like Bryan McMahon, J.B. Keane, Professor Brendan Kennelly and, of course, the famous Kerry balladier and poet Sean McCarthy – Sean of the stories and the craic. A well-travelled man, Sean was the very embodiment of the saying, 'You can take a man out of the country, but you can't take the country out of the man.' In his life we shared many a laugh; facing his death, I hid my tears.

I remember a great American friend of Sean's once bought a pub in the town of Castleisland, and as I was in nearby Dingle at the time, he invited me over for the opening. On the night, I arrived with a few friends; Sean, coming out to meet me, greeted me with the words: 'I don't mind buying you a drink, Billy, but by Christ I'm not buying any drink for your bloody Dublin Jackeens.' Then, as an afterthought: 'Oh, Billy, would you have a few bob on yeh? I'll fix up with you in the morning.' And no better man; Sean and I borrowed money off each other so often that we never knew who owed what to whom.

Once inside, we discovered that the three best seats were occupied by the new landlord's American friends, all male. The sofa they sat on was plonked down right in front of a big turf fire; due to the size of the poor sofa's three occupants, we latecomers were excluded, not only from the view of the leaping flame, but also from its heat. It was early October, and a fine white frost had invaded the empty streets outside. Rubbing my hands together, I eyed the three men with a certain amount of contempt, muttering that I hoped that, on the Last Day, they wouldn't be sitting as near to Old Nick's fire as they were to that one – but it made no difference: all my ill-mannered remarks were met with blank stares.

'No matter,' said Sean, from his perch against the bar. 'Maybe later on the three gentlemen might oblige the company with a bar or two of an oul' song.' But, as the night wore on in fiddle-playing, music, song and verse, the three gentlemen obliged no one: they remained sitting, free from drink or movement of any kind.

Having accepted that we were not going to dislodge them from the sofa, Sean, being Sean, whispered to me, 'Let's see who'll make them laugh.'

'That's a good idea,' I said. 'It'll show if they're still alive.'

'And, to make it interesting,' said Sean, 'there's a pound note that says I'll be the one to make them laugh.'

'I'll cover that pound note with one of my own,' I said quickly, not wanting to let the Dubs down. But, of course, when I reflected on it later, I had been too hasty: both the pounds now lying on the counter were mine.

We tossed a coin to see who'd go first. I won, but decided to let Sean go first. I thought I had done the wrong thing, because Sean's opening words made everyone within earshot stop talking: 'When I was a wee lad, winter and summer I walked over the hills to school in my bare feet.' In the silence that greeted his words, one could almost hear a violin.

'Terrible times, terrible times,' muttered a well-dressed woman with a cigarette in one hand and a very big Johnny Walker whiskey in the other. 'I don't know how we survived, honest to God I don't.'

'Aye,' Sean continued, 'things were rough and things were tough. We hadn't even a goat to milk. I remember I had to come in from school, grab the milk can and walk two miles down the railway line to oul' Murphy's dairy yard. Well, one day I arrived at the yard only to be met by Mr Murphy himself, a very tall man.'

Sean, a true storyteller, paused to sip his pint before continuing. '"Come here, you," said Murphy. "What are you doin' here in my yard?"

'"I've come for the milk, sir," said I.

'"Have yeh, now? And what would be your name, boy?" he asked.

'"McCarthy, sir."

'"There's a million McCarthys around here. Which one are you?"

'"From Dirrha Bog, sir."'

As Sean was speaking, I looked quickly around the pub.

Everyone was listening intently to the story – everyone but the three old boys sitting on the sofa, who still sat as if set in plaster.

'"You're a McCarthy from Dirrha Bog, you say?" he repeated.

'"Yes, sir," I replied, thinking that my good manners had impressed him.' Sean reached for his pint again. '"Well, McCarthy," says tall Mr Murphy, bending down so that his red face was level with mine, "tell your father that two of my cows that were sick died this morning; and also tell him, young McCarthy of Dirrha Bog, that he owes me for milk dating back for ten years. Now, on your feckin' bike, before I have another heart attack."'

'My God! What happened then?' asked the lady with the large whiskey and the cigarette.

'Well,' continued Sean, 'I came home and put the empty can on the table. Around sunset, me father comes in and puts the can to his lips; then a look of surprise comes over his face. "Where's the milk, Seaneen?" he asks. "There's no milk, Da," says I. "Oul' Mr Murphy said that two of his cows that were sickening died this morning, and he also said you owe him for ten years' milk."'

'And what did your father say?' asked the new owner of the pub.

'Well,' answered Sean, after putting a match to the bowl of his pipe and drawing the smoke into his mouth, 'the Da was so clever with figures, he should have been in the government. "Put your cap back on, Seaneen," says he, "and go down and close the account!"'

Of course, this caused great and loud laughter in the pub – among everyone, that is, but the three old gentlemen still sitting on the sofa. Not so much as a titter escaped their lips. So I knew it was down to me. As the prolonged laughter died away, I spoke up: 'On the way here from Dingle this evening, we stopped at an oul' shebeen of a pub –'

'Where was this pub?' inquired Sean, stopping me in full flight. 'I know most of the shebeens from here to the town of Dingle.'

'Well, you don't know this one,' I replied. 'And I'll thank you, Sean McCarthy, not to interrupt me, for I never did it to you.'

'Point taken,' said Sean, winking at me. 'You've the floor.'

Ignoring him, I continued, 'As I was saying, on our way here we stopped at this oul' shebeen of a pub, for no better reason than that I wanted to go to the toilet. "Where's the toilet?" I asked the man behind the counter. "Oh, down the back yard, sir," he replied, busy handing out bottles of very black stout to some of my party.

'Well, obeying his directions, I arrived outside a small shed with its door neither open nor closed, due to the fact that it was buried deep in muck. Inside I found little but a big bucket almost full of excreta, guarded by a mountain of flies. Delighted that my call of nature only necessitated the use of my kidneys, I quickly relieved myself and joined my good companions again at the bar.

'Well, just as I was drinking my bottle of stout by the neck, who should come into the pub but three middle-aged Americans. Two of them immediately sat down on the sofa in front of the fire.' I paused for effect. I need not have bothered, for all eyes were now focused on the sofa and its three still occupants. '"Say, landlord," inquired the one Yank who was still standing, "would you have a toilet in this establishment?" The barman replied, as he had to me, "Oh, down the back yard, sir."'

At this stage I reached for my pipe; but, seeing the look of anticipation on the eager faces around me, I decided to forego the pleasure of the pipe and continue my story.

'As I was saying, from my place at the bar I could see this rather fat American gentleman make his way slowly down the yard. Having reached the door, he tried and tried to lift it out of the soft mud until, like King Bruce with the spider, he succeeded.'

'What happened then?' asked a fair-haired young girl with an English accent.

'Well, after being inside the loo for about ten minutes, he emerged with his belt around his neck, tucking his shirt into his trousers as he arrived back in the pub. "Landlord," he said, "do you know that there's no lock on the inside of your toilet door?"

'"Not to worry," said the barman. "It's been that way thirty years and we haven't lost a bucket of shit yet."'

My story was greeted with great laughter by everyone but the three old Americans sitting on the sofa. It was as if their souls had already left their bodies and, being in the wilds of Kerry, had lost their way.

Someone suggested a hymn, so the lady with the Johnny Walker and the cigarette led us in 'Show me the way to go home' and other tunes that had us crying into our beer. As Sean remarked, 'It was one hell of a wake.'

CHAPTER 12

Four Men with Funny Faces

In the 50s, a journeyman's lot was not an easy one. Jobs were hard to come by, and those of us who were lucky enough to have a job had to travel great distances. One had to clock in on site at 8.30am, so I, living in Crumlin, often had to leave the house before 7.30am to cycle the seven or eight miles to Finglas or beyond. For this was how Dublin Corporation was attempting to solve its acute housing problems: they would buy up huge tracts of land, then parcel them out to a few select builders, who would attempt to build the number of houses allocated to them and hand them over to the Corporation well before the specified deadline.

This was nearly always achieved on the bent backs of the workers, and there were many ways this was done. For instance, first thing every Monday morning, there were always several men outside the gate looking for a job. The trades foreman would start most of them; but at about ten o'clock, he would go up to all of them but one and say, 'You, you, you and you – you're no effin' use to me, so you can clear off the site.'

Now it has to be said that a lot of so-called 'tradesmen' looking for work didn't really know their trade. Many carpenters, in particular, had come back from England, where they had simply done a quick course in carpentry, and, to be frank, they were only wood-butchers. It was the same with some plumbers – 'wavin-fixers' (wavin is a light material used instead of copper or lead piping) who wouldn't know how to bend a bit of copper or seal a lead joint. Even my own trade did not escape these new quick-fixers. Overnight, adverts for blocklayers, as opposed to bricklayers, appeared in most papers; and the blocks that we were laying suddenly increased in size from four inches by nine by eighteen to six inches by nine by eighteen. They were huge masses of solid concrete, weighing in at around five stone each; trying to lift these monsters from the ground to chest-height caused many a good bricklayer to retire and even die. It took several years of work by the Guild before those responsible for creating those monsters finally gave in to our demands and abolished them. It was said, about this time, that you never saw an old bricklayer on a site; they only looked old from lifting those bloody six-inch blocks.

Also around this time the real brick, which is burnt in a kiln, almost disappeared from use, except in churches and other such buildings. In my young day there were a lot of small, and not so small, brickfields, like the local Mount Argus and Dolphin's Barn brickfields. They turned out bricks that were uniformly made – that is, they all measured exactly the same; these were known as 'pressed' bricks, because they were made by pressing suitably prepared clay or shale into steel moulds before firing them in the kiln. But, with the high cost of producing these and other bricks (like 'wire-cut' and 'hand-made' bricks), the building fathers suddenly rediscovered sand and cement, thus spawning the blocklayer.

When we were young, my father always taught us budding young bricklayers that every wall, irrespective of height or thickness, should be non-political – that is, it should lean neither to the right nor to the left. But it has to be said a lot of these blocklayers' political leanings were all over the place, their use of plumb rules was non-existent, and most of them didn't even bother to wipe the 'snots' of mortar off the wall. Their cry, 'The plaster will cover it,' became a slogan for bad workmanship.

They also spawned a building joke that went the rounds at that time. It appears that this old lady wanted a garden wall built; but, hearing that some builders tried to baffle clients with jargon, she decided to read up on some of the rules of bonding bricks together. When the builder announced that the wall was completed, she went out to look at it – and discovered that the wall had a large belly in it. 'It doesn't look straight to me,' cried the old lady. 'Are you sure it's plumb?' 'Plumb?' shouted the blocklayer. 'Madam, I should be charging you extra – I'll have you know it's *over* plumb!'

And so, between many untrained building operatives and some 'get it up at all costs' building foremen, a uneasy peace settled on most sites, with us regular tradesmen and the hoxies caught in the middle. As I have already stated, these hoxies were highly skilled in almost all sections of building work. But, with the introduction of wavin pipes, the laying of sewerage pipes became easier and quicker; doing away with the large timber poles for scaffolding and replacing them with steel poles and fittings took the real creative skill away; pre-cast lintels did the same. Every type of work that the hoxie had taken pride in doing was now being done by men with very little experience and no tradition behind them.

In our frustration with conditions on sites, the foreman became the enemy. From our point of view, this was the only attitude we could adopt. Firstly, we were away from home for long hours – often ten or more – each day; and, because there were no canteen facilities on sites in those days, we had to exist on a few sandwiches and uncertain brews of tea, while doing very hard and heavy work. Also, there was no guarantee that, when we arrived on site, we were going to get a day's work: frosty or wet weather could put a stop to work. To combat this, the government brought in a scheme for 'wet time'. We building workers were forced to contribute to this scheme on a weekly basis. But the mere pittance that was paid back to us if any of us were unfortunate enough to suffer 'wet time' (and the bricklayers were the main sufferers) did not take into consideration two things: firstly, we were not responsible for the rain, snow or frost; and, secondly, why should our wives and children have had to suffer a drop in their standard of daily living because some faceless people in their guaranteed jobs in Social Welfare had set the payouts far below our living wage?

So, as always when the seeds of discontent are sown, it all too quickly became 'them and us'. This unrest manifested itself, not in refusals to work – for that would have meant instant dismissal, and rightly so – but in more subtle ways.

In those days the 'ganger' – the charge-hand supervising the labourers – was often an ex-policeman or a retired army sergeant, and many of them suffered from the illusion that they were still in their respective Forces. Instead of respecting the labourers for what they were – highly intelligent people, who would have responded with greater interest and with suggestions if the job in hand had been explained to them – the gangers simply shouted, 'You, you and you – follow me!' Most gangers – I won't say all – were appointed because they were able to shout loudly. The times were such that most builders, and especially general foremen, loved to hear the men shouted at. Some of these foremen and gangers often could not explain a particular job to the men under them, for the simple reason that they had very little knowledge of how to go about it themselves; so most of them just stood over the men until they completed the job. Then these same foremen or gangers muttered about the length of time it had taken to do it.

I was always fascinated by one ganger who was on the same site as myself, over on the north side of the city. Presumably because he was constantly shouting at men out of the corner of his mouth, this man's mouth had actually moved until it was almost permanently set between his nose and his ear. I would stare at him as, his eyes closed, he bellowed out his instructions to the poor devils under him, and I'd wonder: when he was at home at night, having his evening meal, did his wife pour out his tea into a cup, or did she just simply pour it into his ear? Such insane thoughts kept me from going mad in that asylum some men called the workplace.

On the same site was a carpenter foreman who was a despicable type. Whereas most foremen wore clothes that made them easily identifiable, this character removed his coat and, donning a dirty old cap, mingled with the men; so any man foolish enough not to look over his shoulder before making disparaging remarks about the job or the foreman soon found himself, bag and cabbage, outside the gate. I remember one particular day: it was cloudy, with rain at times, and Kevin Hanly and I were delighted to be inside one of the houses, building the four-inch solid walls. Kevin was a lovely bricklayer and a soulmate – that is, we shared the same kind of quirky humour.

'There goes the little fecker,' said Kevin, pointing with his trowel through one of the window openings. Looking out, I was just in time to spot this obnoxious little man climbing the large ladder that led up to the point where two older carpenters were putting the large roof-thrusts together.

'Have yeh any loose nails in there?' The voice startled me. Turning, I saw it was the nipper, who, in his spare time, had to go around the site picking up any discarded nails and other such small fittings that he might come across.

Looking skyward, I noticed that the clouds were gathering, promising a real haymaker of a shower; so, thinking of the foreman up on the roof in his shirt-sleeves, I spoke sharply to the nipper. 'I'm glad I saw you. I was told to tell you to take that ladder over there and bring it up to the top of the site – they're waiting on it.'

'Who told yeh I was to do it?' the young fellow asked.

'I don't know – there's more bosses around here... I don't know his name – a big fella, he was. "Tell the nipper," he said, "to bring that ladder up there as soon as possible."'

Kevin, quickly sizing up the situation, shouted at the young fellow, 'Are you not gone yet? There'll be hell to pay if you don't get going with that ladder.' The poor young fellow dropped his nail-box, ran out and, with the kind help of a young apprentice painter, unhooked the large aluminium ladder and carried it away to the top of the site.

A very short time later, large drops of rain signalled the start of the father and mother of all showers. It was the kind of fierce deluge that could only be enjoyed if one was in a building with a roof on it, looking out at an almost demented foreman realising that the ladder he had been about to descend was no longer there.

His first reaction was to call over to us, 'Hey, you two, get me a ladder and be bloody quick about it!'

Not getting a reaction, he started to shout loudly in a tinny voice. Of course, by then we two bricklayers had become very conscientious: we were busy laying four-inch solid blocks, and of course we didn't hear the shouts until they had developed into a scream. Then big Kevin paused and listened as a nature-lover would on hearing the first cuckoo. He said, 'Hey, Billy, do you hear someone singing?'

'Could be that big fat plumber two houses up; I hear he's getting his voice trained,' I replied. I headed out the back, followed by Kevin, who remarked that the worst of the rain seemed to be over.

All this time the roaring continued, as the foreman, now

bove: My dad and me in O'Connell Street, Christmas Eve, 1932.

bove: First Holy Communion, 1934.

ight: Outside Crumlin Post Office in '944 with Dick Shaugessy (left) and ny brother Brendan (right).

Above: Pushing a handcart through the streets of Dublin was never an easy job. (Courtesy of The Irish Historical Picture Company.)

Right: Bricklayers' Guildhall, Cuffe Street.

lbove: Granby Lane, Dublin – Matt Talbot died here. (Courtesy of The rish Historical Picture Company.)

lbove: My father working as a bricklayer in Captain's Lane, Crumlin, in the 1950s. Tommy Lawlor is on he right.

Right: 'Cyclone' Bill Warren, one of the best heavyweight fighters of the early 1900s. (Courtesy of Terry O'Neill.)

Above: My brother Johnny (right) working on site in Perth, Australia.

Right: My brother Brendan (right) working in Kent, England.

Left: Dress dance at the Metropole in Dublin in the 1950s.

ight: Maeve and myself on O'Connell treet Bridge, 1951.

elow: Painting by Maeve French.

Left: The poet Seán McCarthy

Right: Former President Patrick Hillery with Bryan McMahon.

Left: Me with some of the workers in the Killeen Paper Mills in 1950.

bove: Judd Brothers Iide & Skin Works, where I once worked with Eddie Steel. This uilding was later estroyed by fire. Courtesy of The Irish Iistorical Picture ompany.)

ight: A group of illeen workers at one f our Christmas arties, 1958. I'm on he extreme left.

Left: Maeve and me at my retirement party in 1992.

Right: Some retirement! Hard at work building a barbecue.

nearly demented, danced up and down on the very narrow platform trying to attract our attention. Of the two elderly carpenters, there was no sign; they must have silently disappeared into some sheltered spot known only to themselves. As we stood outside and the rain finally eased, Kevin took up the thread of my last remark. 'You were saying that screaming could be coming from the big fat plumber?'

'Yes – he's into opera in a big way, so I'm told by his mate,' I said. The two of us were very careful to look everywhere except in the direction of the dishevelled, near-drowned figure still shouting hoarsely in our direction.

'Well, all I can say is he must have been trained by someone down in Australia,' remarked Kevin. 'Because that noise could only be coming from his arse.'

It was then I spotted the nipper and the young apprentice struggling down through the muck with the ladder on their shoulders. 'Oh, Christ, we've had it now,' I whispered to Kevin. 'Here's the bloody ladder back.'

But I had reckoned without Kevin's ability to think on his feet. Looking up at the foreman, he called out, 'Are you looking for a ladder to get down, sir?'

As the now-near-mummified figure nodded his head, Kevin turned to me. 'Don't stand there – hurry up, man! We'll have to go and get a ladder for the foreman to get down.' He winked at me, and we both charged over to the two young lads struggling with the ladder. 'Here, we'll take that ladder; you two lads look half done in.'

The nipper peered at me. 'Wasn't it you who told us to take this bloody ladder up to the top of the site?'

'No,' I lied. 'It must have been my brother. Anyhow, we'll take it off your hands now.'

Before the two poor young lads had a chance to say anything else, we grabbed the ladder and almost ran with it to the base of the platform. 'Here's the ladder, sir, like we promised.'

It must have been a full ten minutes before the foreman felt strong enough to descend to the ground, helped by our encouraging shouts of 'Mind the step, sir,' 'Tread carefully, sir,' and other such considerate remarks. As his feet hit the ground at last, we rushed to help him, only to be brushed aside. His teeth were chattering and he was nearly drowned. Placing his face within a few inches of ours, he whispered, 'Are you two effers deaf?'

Then, huddled into himself and for the first time stripped of his arrogance, this pathetic little man staggered away, watched only by his two rescuers.

CHAPTER 13

Father and Son

Once again I was on the move. The site was different, but the buildings were the same type that I had spent the last couple of years working on: mass-produced concrete houses for Dublin Corporation. The only jobs for the brickies were the downstairs concrete walls, the two-inch breeze walls upstairs, the spud-stones, laying out the sewerage systems, and laying out, forming and gathering in the four fireplace openings.

This is a back-breaking job; it requires a vast amount of blocks so that you can, at the completion of the job, gather them all in to form one chimney-stack with four flue-liners projecting evenly over the finished stack. Most sites in those days had only a pulley rope; a man below strapped the block to this pulley and hauled it up, and another man took it and carried it over to where four of us stood waiting. It was all right if the weather was good, but it was no joke if you were waiting thirty feet or more up in cold winter winds, doing nothing and trying to keep warm. The mortar was placed in a bucket and arrived the same way. On some sites, you might get a hoxie who was a hod-carrier; he would fill his hod with a couple of stone of mixed mortar, or two or more blocks, and carry it all the way up the ladders to you. The hod was made of heavy timber and was supported by a very thick pole, about five feet in height, which allowed the hod-carrier to get underneath and carry it.

These were horses of men, doing work horses couldn't and wouldn't do. Due to the nature of their work, most of these gentlemen went to their reward in the next world before their allotted time on this earth was up. May they rest in peace, for in this life they saw very little of the good times.

Of course, in their own way they were crafty devils: when they arrived on the scaffolding, they would always pick up the fastest brickie's trowel and, under cover of cleaning out the hod, start telling some story or other that went on and on. One particular hod-carrier – who had developed duck's feet (feet that turned right out) from constantly climbing ladders – was forever telling us about his brother in England, who had made a success of his life and was buying into the ballroom business over there. 'Do you know,' he'd say, at the same time holding on to one of our lads' trowels, 'that the brother has one of the biggest ballrooms in London?'

Which caused the owner of the trowel to explode with the caustic remark, 'Be Jaysus, if he has feet like yours he'd need all the extra space he can get just to turn.'

But rude remarks were completely ignored by this particular hoxie, who, while still holding on to the brickie's trowel, would tell you again about the first time he went to work in England.

'"What are you?" the foreman asked me,' he'd say.

'"I'm an all-round man, sir," I replied.

'"Yes, but what do you specialise in?" inquired he.

'"I'm a hod-carrier," says I.

'"That's bloody great," says he, "I'm short of a hod-carrier. Can you start right away?"

'"OK," says I. "I'll just take off my coat and hang it up in that shed there."

'"What shed?" said the foreman, looking puzzled.

'"That large shed there in front of us, sir," I said, pointing it out to him.

'"That's not a shed, Paddy. That's the bloody hod."'

In the early 50s, modern machinery and labour-saving devices had not yet arrived at a lot of building sites in Ireland; men who had worked in England loved to come back and tell you about the strange and wonderful machinery and modern methods they had encountered 'across the pond' – notwithstanding the fact that most of us had already been there and had experienced these newfangled things ourselves.

I remember quite clearly a man telling me about the time he first went to England to work. 'When was this?' I asked him – for this Dublin character was known as a real spoofer.

'During the Battle of Britain,' said he, sucking a cigarette butt, which in some strange way helped him to lapse back in time. '1940, it was; times were grim.'

'Did you see any of the dogfights between the planes?' I asked.

'Did I see any dogfights? Not 'alf I didn't.'

It never ceased to amaze me how some men, when telling you a story of something that happened to them over in England, suddenly and without any explanation always adopt a Cockney way of speaking. I think they really believe it adds a touch of authenticity to their unbelievable stories.

'Terrible times – terrible times,' he muttered. 'Jerry was comin' over every hour on the hour. "Blimey," I remember sayin' to myself, "our boys in blue can't stick much more of this."'

'You knew the Battle of Britain pilots personally, then?' This sarcastic remark came from a tall, thin, rather delicate-looking painter, who had a habit of staring into space while talking. Much later, I found out that he had been a rear-gunner in a Royal Air Force plane shot down over Germany, and had spent three years of his young life in a prison camp.

'Well, of course, not all of them, like,' answered the spoofer.

'How did you know them?' I inquired.

'Wasn't I working in Biggin Hill airfield in Kent? Yes, I seen them all, mate – includin' Bader, the legless wonder. Many the time he'd call to me, "Hey, Paddy, me oul' pal, lift me out of this bloody wheelchair and put me in my Spit so I can chase them blasted Jerries back from our lovely English shores."'

'You served in the RAF, then?'

'No – not really served in them, as such.'

'But you said you worked at Biggin Hill.'

'So I did.'

'Doing what?'

Then, and only then, our spoofer looked a bit uncomfortable. 'Filling in holes,' he muttered. Then, brightening up all of a sudden, he proclaimed, 'We were in the front line, mate. While Jerry was overhead dropping his bombs, we were out there filling in the craters so that our fighter planes could come in to land, be juiced up and take off again to fight the blasted Hun.'

'Your lot must have won a whole lot of medals, then,' muttered the tall painter.

'No, we didn't actually qualify for medals,' replied the spoofer. 'But there was this right eejit of a culchie working with us, and the foreman called him one day and said, "I'll be building a small dug-out, so I want you to dig out a hole measuring twenty feet long and eight feet wide, and go down about ten or twelve feet."

'"On me own, by meself?" asked this gobshite.

'"Of course. I'll be back about four; you should have it dug out by then. I'll arrange for you to get the JCB," said the foreman; then he quickly walked away.

'Well,' said the spoofer, 'this arsehole had never heard of a JCB, let alone driven one as I had. He thought it was some kind of medal, like the Distinguished Service Order or the VC, because at that time the papers would be full of such-and-such a pilot having got the DFC or the DSO for bravery. So when the foreman said he was off to get your man the JCB, this fella shouted after him. "You can keep your effin' JCB and the rest of your bloody medals!" said he. "I'm off back home to Ireland, where, if you're made to work like a horse, at least you can stop now and then to fart like one!'"

The new site I opted for was similar to the one I had left, except for two very important considerations that swayed me to move. Firstly, the new site was situated in the old brickfields, just off the Crumlin Road and only a mile or two from my own house; and, secondly, my father was working on the same site. In all my years as an apprentice and as a fully fledged journeyman, I, like my two brothers, had never worked with him – except on nixers, or 'private jobs', as he liked to call them. So, although I was looking forward to sharing a mortarboard with the Da, I was more than a little apprehensive about how I'd shape up to his very high standards.

This new site was set up slightly differently from the other local government housing sites I had worked on. Because it was a direct labour scheme organised by Dublin Corporation themselves, they had taken the trouble to hand-pick their top supervisors very carefully. The general foreman was a Cavan man by the name of Mr O'Reilly, and the brickie foreman was Dan McConnall, whom I had worked under in Bushy Park. He was tough but fair, and very knowledgeable about all aspects of the building game; when I first worked under him, he had taught me a great deal about bricklaying and the building game in general.

Working with the Da was, for me, a strange experience. Reflecting on it now, in the gentleness of time, I know I was more than just lucky: I was blessed – not only in being the beneficiary of his considerable knowledge as a bricklayer, but also in sharing eight hours a day with him and in finding out that he wasn't just the Da, but also a very caring, very human man.

This trait revealed itself in many small ways that, when added up, gave you the measure of the man. For instance, one day I noticed that he had eaten his sandwiches very quickly (normally he was a very slow eater), so I offered him one of mine, which Maeve, my wife, had cut for me that morning. But he declined with a smile, saying, 'Your mother would be asking me what was in them, and no matter what I said, she'd make some remark or other about them and then I'd feel I was the cause of it.'

It would never have occurred to him to say nothing to her about the sandwiches; they were a very close couple who discussed everything. One of my abiding memories of my childhood is of seeing my father and mother going into the kitchen every Friday night, when he came home from work; they would lay out his wages on the table, and the two of them would work out who and what had to be paid that week – a habit that my own wife and I continue to this day.

Then there were the times when he made me cringe with acute embarrassment. It was a well-known fact that he hated bad language, and when one of the lads would inject a few colourful words into the conversation, my father would look at him hard before asking, 'Does that make you a bigger man?' And poor me, not knowing where to look!

On this site, as on all building sites the world over, there was this character who religiously, every Monday morning, borrowed a half-crown off my father; then, when Friday came along and he got paid, he'd make a big thing of handing the Da back his half-crown. One Friday, after a few weeks of this, when the Da received the half-crown from this character in front of everyone, he handed it back to him and said, 'Here, Joe. It's getting to the point where I don't know if it's you or I who owns this half-crown, so you'd better keep it.' Joe never troubled him again.

My father's strong principles and good-natured kindness

must have been the only legacies he inherited from his dear mother, a lady who lived and died young, in a tenement room in an old part of Dublin commonly known as the Liberties. The Liberties are so named because of a visit King Henry VIII paid to Dublin city. As he stood on the high walls overlooking St Audoen's Gate, on a market day, he noticed a lot of people selling their livestock, farm produce and other wares outside the city gates. 'Why are those people selling their wares outside the gate, instead of inside the walls?' he asked the Lord Mayor. The Lord Mayor replied, 'Because they refuse to pay the city tax, Your Majesty.' It may have been one of those in-between times when Henry was thinking of getting rid of the old and acquiring a younger bit of stuff; but, whatever the reason, it is on record that he turned and said to the Lord Mayor, 'I, Henry, give them the liberty to stay there.'

And they did, in rat-infested tenements that housed anything up to eight families. They stayed, the women because it was near their chapel and their neighbours, the men because of the nearness of the mother and the pubs. For drink was the cushion that deadened all pain and ambition.

My grandfather, old Ha'-pa'-nine, was, I suppose, a man of his own time. He worked hard when he could get work – which wasn't very often – and he drank hard when he could get drink, which, at the low prices, was very often. And he never overburdened his sons or daughters with any signs of love or affection. I suppose his heart only generated enough love to keep him sane. In the times that were in it, these men seemed satisfied to settle into the slot that their so-called 'betters' had allocated to them. It was my father's generation who, having survived first a World War and then a civil war, started the long struggle for some kind of equality for all people.

In those days, building jobs often took years to complete. My father's eldest brother, Jack, who was killed in the First

World War, served his full six years' apprenticeship working on a military barracks in Dublin.

While working out in Dun Laoghaire, my grandfather, after a night's drinking, would often insist that my father, who was at that time about twelve years of age, should follow him out to the building site with his lunch. This meant my father had to miss school and hike the seven long miles there and back in all weathers. One time, he told me, coming back tired and hungry, he spotted a shop outside of which was a large display of fruit. Seeing nobody about, he quickly grabbed an apple and ran like the devil himself was after him. The following Saturday at his weekly confession, when he told the priest what he had done, the priest said to him, 'I am only giving you absolution on the condition that you make restitution.'

There the Da stopped to light a cigarette and looked at me. 'Do you know what, son?' he said. 'I was nearly twenty years of age before I found out what the word "restitution" meant.' Then, with that smile that was never too far from his face, he whispered, 'So the way I figure it is, your grandfather, oul' Ha'-pa'-nine, was directly responsible for me stealing and missing school; and if, when I die, I'm billed with robbing that apple, I'll just say to St Peter, "Pete, old boy, I'm afraid this time you've really got the wrong boy."'

I soon found that working with the Da was a real joy. Looking back now, across the great distance of time, I know I was enriched by his quiet and steady commitment to those firm principles that seem to have slowly gone out of fashion in all walks of life – principles like honesty, decency, and respect for your fellow man. And I amazed myself by listening and learning from the da as he shared the tricks of the trade with me, even though I was a fully fledged brickie. I remember him showing me the proper way to lay out a fireplace and chimney-stack. Because most of this work was hidden and the exterior covered up by the plasterer, there was a tendency among some brickies to take short-cuts on some of the essentials. But not the Da: from the setting out of the blocks to the spacing of the final flues, his aim was to create the perfect job. I believe that in this he was helped, not only by his own years of experience, but by the many generations of bricklayers in his family before him who had finely honed this skill.

I also discovered that, while actually engaged in building, my father always whistled or even sang softly to himself – contemporary songs that he would immediately term 'rubbish' if he caught any of us listening to them on Radio Luxembourg or any of the other pirate radio stations that we, the younger generation, tended to listen to at that time.

This habit of whistling or singing softly to oneself while laying bricks was quite commonplace among the older generation of workers – with, of course, many variations. Paddy 'the Lumper' Cullen and his brother Andy were two of the neatest and sweetest bricklayers you'd meet on a day's walk. Andy, the quieter of the two, would just smile at you when things were going right; but Paddy, if he saw any foreman standing nearby, would sing as he laid the bricks, 'Oh, my baby needs new shoes, oh, baby does... baby needs new shoes, oh, baby does...'

CHAPTER 14

The Unholy Talk in Church

The last job I worked on with my father was Walkinstown Church. The builder was Hetherington and Sons, the firm I had started serving my time with in 1943. Now, in 1955, there I was working for them once again; the only difference was that I was now a fully fledged journeyman, married and the father of a beautiful little girl.

It was a happy job. This was partly because of the general foreman's vast knowledge of church work and his attitude to the men: he treated us as human beings and gave full rein to our own individual styles of working. But, reflecting on it over the years, I have come to realise that Eddie Hetherington wasn't just a nice man; he was very much more than that. He was the sort of man other men followed with confidence and without question.

This is a great gift, which most men in authority seek to attain but very few ever do. It requires a few known ingredients: real knowledge of the work you are asking others under you to carry out, a certain tact that will allow the dissatisfied worker to think that he has brought the supervisor around to his way of thinking, and, above all, an honesty that must always appear transparent. Now, these ingredients can be and are taught in supervisors' courses; but, like most streamlined big-business seminars that intend to create that perfect output, these courses turn out supervisors who are each an exact replica of the one gone before – because they simply lack that unknown ingredient that our Maker plants in very few hearts. I am speaking of charisma, an almost undefinable thing.

Strange, but the few men I have met who possessed this inexplicable quality were also very handsome men, and Eddie Hetherington was no exception. Another such man was Donal O'Reilly, a foreman plasterer in the direct labour scheme that my father and I had just packed in so we could work on the new Walkinstown Church. Donal, like Eddie Hetherington, had that very rare quality of being able to get the best out of his men; and, stranger still, the workmen on his site felt a certain pride in being called 'his' men – even though this sometimes meant being asked to do that bit extra beyond the terms of their employment.

Eddie and Donal were completely different in outlook and temperament, but both liked guns. Eddie loved nothing better than to walk the lands near Blessington in the early morning, looking for all kinds of game, while Donal's whole background centred around guns of one kind or another. Born and nurtured in a Republican family, Donal always claimed he was the first casualty of the 1916 Rising. A very close and very dear relation of his was a member of the Irish Citizen Army, and when he marched behind James Connolly into the GPO on that fateful Easter Monday morning, the very young Donal was inspired to join him. As Donal loved to explain: 'I was only in the door when Commandant-General James Connolly caught me by the scruff of the neck and, propelling me towards the door, told me to be a good boy and go home to me mammy. Then, without any more ado, this great man helped me on my way by giving me a foot in the arse.' Donal would say, laughing, 'Sure, didn't that make me the first casualty of the Rebellion?'

This jovial front that Donal presented acted as a kind of shield for the man's real feelings, which had led him to join the national movement as a young man and later, in 1936, to follow Frank Ryan to Spain as part of that first truly social movement, the International Brigade. Another member of that famous Brigade was our very own Bill Scott, who always loved to give his address as 'The Ancient Guild of Incorporated Brick and Stonelayers' Union, 49 Cuffe Street, Dublin'. Looking back, with the great advantage of hindsight, over that period and its unfolding of huge historic events, I feel I was very privileged and honoured to have known and worked with such men.

Our reason for leaving the direct labour scheme was twofold. Firstly, my father, who always had his ear to the ground, had heard from a very reliable source that there was soon going to be a large lay-off of men, which would flood the work market in the Dublin area. Such were the conditions in the building trade at that time that, anxious to work and provide for your family, you always tried to keep at least two steps in front of unemployment, and this was done by now and then looking over your shoulder and planning your next move. For these were terrible times. Until the 50s we had over one thousand bricklayers in Dublin and the surrounding area, but during the following decade we lost over half of these men through emigration. My own two brothers were among them: Johnny went to Australia and Brendan to London. These lads, and five hundred more, never came back home to work in Ireland again.

The other reason we left the direct labour scheme was the repetitive nature of the work. After working on public housing schemes over a period of some years, one eventually found a rust forming on one's creative powers; this brought a fear of losing one's touch – a very real fear that only tradesmen and other creative people can understand. So, when the opportunity presented itself, my Da and I both opted to work on Walkinstown Church.

It was great to work with brick and stone again, even though all the stone was pre-cut. The bricks were from Cavan, and, as the saying goes, some were more uniform than others, causing us to take that extra care in making and keeping our perps (the vertical joints between bricks) straight. As I have already stated, it was a happy site, with only one drawback, and that was the weather. As it was a church job, there was no inside work, for the roof could not be formed until all the walls were up – and, of course, the day all the walls were completed, the bricklayer's work was done.

There is a lot of truth in the old story of the two women meeting, and one asking the other what her husband worked at.

'He's a bricklayer,' answered the second woman.

'Oh, I hear they earn great money,' said her friend.

'Oh, yes, they earn it all right,' said the brickie's wife with a shake of her head. 'But unfortunately they don't bloody well get it.'

The building site was a great place for yarns, which were usually – but not always – based on truth. I remember a painter telling us a story about how, many years ago, when he was a young fellow, he was working in John's Lane Church in Thomas Street. As he described the scene, I noticed the almost poetic way he painted the setting.

'It was gathering dusk on a late November evening, and, with no lights on, this old painter was trying his best to finish the second undercoat high up over the altar. All of a sudden, this poor woman comes into the church.'

'Why, where were you?' asked one of the plasterers.

'Wasn't I sandpapering down one of those large seats?' the painter said, looking at the interrupter with a beady eye. He continued, 'Right away I could see she was in a very emotional state.'

'How did you know?' This question, like the first one, came from the plasterer, who was just sitting there inspecting his fingernails.

'Wasn't I beside her and heard her sobbing!' replied the painter in an exasperated tone of voice.

'Are you fully satisfied with that answer?' asked Tucker Holohan, directing his question to the plasterer, but winking at the rest of us. We were sitting around trying to keep warm, while the puddles of dirty water from the rain falling outside grew bigger.

'As I was saying before I was so rudely interrupted, this poor woman walked straight up to the main altar and, throwing herself down, cried out in a very loud voice, "Oh, Virgin Mother of God, help me – please help me in my terrible sorrow!"

'Now the old painter, hearing the voice call out below and thinking it was one of us, shouted down, "What do you want? Can't you see I'm busy up here?"'

At this point the painter stopped, waiting for the plasterer to say something; but the plasterer was too busy inspecting his fingernails even to look up. So the painter continued, 'The poor woman, on hearing the man's voice, replied, "It's not you I want, it's your mammy!"'

Shortly after that the plasterer spoke, and he prefaced his tale by saying, 'What I'm goin' to tell you is a true story.' Knowing from experience that this was going to be a long-drawn-out story, I decided to fill my pipe. As I held my match over the top of the pipe, I happened to glance over to where my father was sitting; he looked up at that precise moment and smiled at me, and I, seeing his tired, worn face through that blue haze of smoke, captured that winsome smile forever in my heart.

'When I was a young man in the town of Rathdrum in the county of Wicklow,' said the elderly plasterer, 'there were great missions held in the church – the first week for the women, and the second week for the men.' All heads nodded in agreement, for we all remembered the missions, where fire and brimstone and the burning of souls were the order of the day. 'Well,' the plasterer continued, 'our little church had a wooden pulpit, and the biggest of the two missioners used to thump the pulpit something shocking when he'd be making his point. During one of these fierce attacks on the pulpit, the crowd in the small church started to laugh, and the priest was so annoyed that he walked out of the pulpit and into the vestry, where he complained to the clerk of the church.

'"They laughed at me!" he cried, almost sobbing his words.

'"Oh, no, Father, they weren't laughing at you," said the old clerk, trying to reassure him.

'"But why did they laugh when I banged the pulpit?" demanded the priest.

'"Well, Father, there was a mouse peeping out from a small hole at the base of the pulpit; every time you struck the pulpit he would dart in, and then after a while out he would peep again – until you hit the pulpit again. And of course the people, being what they are, all thought it was very funny."

'The priest was satisfied and delighted that the women of the parish hadn't been laughing at him. But it so happened that, the very next night, didn't someone bring poor Daisy up to the mission.'

'Who was Daisy? Or are we allowed to ask?' Without turning, I knew that the voice could only be the painter's.

'Of course you're allowed to ask,' answered the plasterer, in a tone that said he wasn't too pleased with anyone interrupting him in full flight. 'She was a local character by the name of Daisy Flower.'

'Daisy Flower? That's a daft name, for a start.' The painter nearly spit out the words.

'Of course, that wasn't her real name.'

'Well, then, why was she called Daisy Flower?'

'Because you could always find her lying on some grass bank or another, out of her mind with drink,' shouted the plasterer.

'And are *you* fully satisfied with *that* answer?' asked Tucker, a smile gathering on his lips. The painter nodded, and the plasterer continued.

'The night before, the younger of the two priests had asked the congregation to bring along any wayward sinners, so someone thought of Daisy. They brought her in and put her into a back seat, where poor Daisy, after a short while, fell fast asleep.' The plasterer looked around, then continued, 'Well, that night the big missioner was again in full flight, roaring about hell and banging the pulpit to the sound of his own voice, when Daisy decided she wanted to pass wind. The sound carried itself hither and thither, with such clarity that to those within earshot the fart actually seemed to magnify itself before passing away in a fearful, long-drawn-out moan. The shocked silence that followed was deafening; then it gave way to sniggering, which was very soon followed by almost uncontrollable laughter.

'On hearing this laughter, the priest was for a moment stunned into silence; then, remembering the clerk's words, he said, smiling, "I know what you're all laughing at, but I can assure you I'll have that hole stuffed by morning!"

'The laughter that greeted that remark, I can tell you, followed the poor man as he hastily left the parish of Rathdrum the next morning, to volunteer for missionary work in darkest Africa. Daisy Flower lived on well into her ninetieth year, unaware that the natives of Africa owed her a debt of gratitude for sending them one more Irish missionary.'

When the church was nearing completion, I was sent by the building firm to help renovate and rebuild an old house in Harold's Cross, Dr Merrick's home. There was a lot of brick used, it being herringbone bond. I remember that, due to the nature of the ground, we had to take extra care to stop moisture percolating through from the base of the wall. The clerk of works said to me, 'Make sure, when you place your DPC [damp-proof course] on the rising wall, that it's perfectly dry underneath.' I pointed out to him that I had recently worked on a school where the clerk of works had told me to make sure I bedded the DPC in sand and cement before laying any bricks on it. 'What's proper – your way or his?' I asked, for I was always keen to learn new ways.

Then he gave me a bit of advice I've carried with me ever since: 'When in doubt, use your own instincts.'

One day, a great friend of mine by the name of Jim Brophy called to my house to tell me that there was a job going in Killeen Paper Mills. They were going to build a power station, and I could get a few weeks' work with no wet time. Jim's words reminded me of a song my father used to sing when I was young:

There'll be something that's nice on the table,
And something that's strong in the tay,
All the world will be bright, next Saturday night,
When McGee draws his first week's pay!

CHAPTER 15

The Killeen Years

Killeen Paper Mill was situated between the townlands of Clondalkin and Ballyfermot, and, like Saggart, Clondalkin and Drimnagh Paper Mills, it was fed by the Camac River. I soon found out that water played a very big part in the making of paper. It was estimated that each mill, having taken in a certain amount of water at the initial stage of paper-making, tended to return at least ninety per cent of it back into the river. It was also said that the Camac River waters were ideally suited to the making of paper – hence the fact that the four paper mills were strategically placed along its banks.

There was little competition between the different mills. Saggart Mill made a very good type of white paper, as well as a very special paper that was used in the making of banknotes and such-like; Clondalkin Mill produced very good types of white and brown paper that were used in commercial and government offices; Killeen Mill produced a very good wrapping paper and, having a first-class corrugated plant, was able to supply corrugated paper and cardboard to all sections of industry; and Drimnagh Mill picked up the slack, as the saying goes. My own mother worked in Drimnagh Paper Mill during the First World War. But, with the widespread use of plastic material after the Second World War, paper-making started to decline; and, unfortunately for those that worked there, Drimnagh Mill was the first to bite the dust.

Of course, all this was unknown to me as I untied my level and tools from my bicycle and presented myself to Mr Holtom, one of the engineers, who checked my credentials and accepted that I was indeed a brickie. I gave him these credentials orally, for it was not the custom at that time for bricklayers to carry any kind of written references indicating where they had worked or what type of experience they had. After a short chat, Mr Holtom directed me to the draughtsman's office, where I met Mr Jim Callaghan and Mr Paddy O'Brien; they showed me the drawings, and then Mr Callaghan came down with me to the site where the power station was to be built of nine-inch cavity blocks.

The job started well for me, with the engineer appointing Jim Brophy as my mate. Little did we know then that we were to work together for six years, in extreme heat, snow and rain – and in all those years, I never once heard Jim use bad language or speak ill of anyone. I asked him about it once, and his reply was: 'Sure, Billy, don't you do enough of it for both of us?'

Like his father before him, Jim was a *piobaire*, a piper who played the uilleann pipes. These Irish pipes differ from the bagpipes in that they have no mouthpiece; the air is forced from a canvas bag placed under the musician's arm. It was always a great wonder to me to see Jim gathering sounds and tone in quick succession and then, with the combination perfectly balanced, producing some wistful, lonely tune that had its roots in a long-vanished Ireland that now lives only in the recesses of the piper's musical mind. It also amazed me that Jim, who never put anything relating to his music down on paper, could carry dozens of these Irish tunes in his head and go effortlessly from one to another – even when he was broadcasting live on RTÉ radio, which he did several times a year.

The power station we were entrusted with building was a

large oblong building designed to house a very sophisticated and highly complicated modern generator. 'This piece of machinery is so sophisticated,' said the German engineer who – with the expert help of Dessie Keogh, the mill's chief electrician – was responsible for assembling it, 'that, when it's up and running, you can place a penny on its edge and it will not move.'

I looked at him and laughed. 'What blind faith you have in the Irish Catholics!'

'What do you mean? I do not understand,' he said.

'The minute you turn around to blow your nose,' I said, 'your penny will have disappeared.'

'You're joking – are you not?' he asked me.

'Put it this way,' I said. 'If you want to prove your theory, by all means put a penny on the edge; but bring more than one penny.'

Later I was proven correct: the penny disappeared and a note signed 'The Irish Magician' was left in its place, while I was left to explain to a rather bewildered German engineer that, according to the Irishman's way of thinking, money, no matter how little, should not be left lying around. Money was for spending; and by this time, I told him, the penny was well and truly spent. The elderly engineer's response was to shake his head in complete bafflement.

The power station itself was a straightforward building job and, with the fine weather, Jim Brophy and I, working well together, made good headway. Towards the end of the third week, we were bedding the last single course. It was a course of nine-inch solids that, when laid, sealed the wall cavity and at the same time added extra strength to take the span forms on which the concrete roof was going to rest. About this time, I had a visitor to the site: Jimmy Garland, who was the resident bricklayer in the mill. He, and his brother Paddy before him, had worked there for a number of years; I knew

Paddy well through his work in the union, but Jimmy was a complete dark horse to me.

'You're doing well.' His authentic Dublin voice drew my attention to him. Looking down, I immediately saw that he was a fellow brickie; it wasn't just his overalls, and the small level and rule in the side pocket – it was something more. Even though his very clean white shirt was off-putting at first, there was something about this rugged man that I immediately liked. Middle-aged, medium height, he was rough and he was tough – and I was to find out over a very short period of time that he was a very determined man who did not suffer fools gladly.

'You're Billy French?' he said, by way of introduction, as I hopped down off the scaffold to meet him. I nodded.

'Paddy speaks well of you,' he half-muttered to himself.

'Aye,' I answered. 'He's a good union man. I heard he was working here in the mill, but left a while ago. Where is he now?'

'Corporation,' Jim answered.

'Corporation?' I repeated. 'That's a bit of a backwater for the likes of your Paddy.' Some jobs suit certain people down to the ground; and yet, no matter how I tried, I could not imagine Paddy Garland being happy stuck on the side of a busy road rebuilding a manhole.

'What do you mean, Billsyer?' asked Jim.

'Your Paddy was always a step above buttermilk – I mean, he liked his cricket and his rugby... I don't think he'll be fulfilled, if you know what I mean, in the Corpo.'

'No, you've got it all wrong, Billsyer. He went in as an inspector.'

'Well, I'm delighted for him. Tell him I wish him well.'

'I will, but I didn't come down to talk about the effin' brother, I came to talk about you.' His voice was stern.

'Me? What about me?'

'You're nearly finished here, so unless you listen to me, you're for the chop on Friday.'

'Well, the Engineer did say there would be only the few weeks' work,' I said. I was prepared for the chop, no matter how unpalatable it was going to be.

'I'm tellin' yeh, if you do as I say, you'll be OK. Don't mind them pen-pushers up there in the office; listen to what I'm tellin' yeh. If the engineer asks you do you know anything about boilers, tell him you know all about Wilson and Lancashire boilers. Do yeh hear me now, Billsyer? Wilsons and Lancashires. Don't forget.'

'Christ, Jim, I wouldn't know one end of a boiler from the other, never mind the names of them.'

'Look, will yeh let me worry about that? You just do as I tell you, and you could be working here for a year or two. Now don't forget – Wilsons and Lancashires.' And then Jim Garland, never one to stand on ceremony, was gone.

The following Friday morning, having bedded the last solid block, I was cleaning my tools with an oily rag when who should appear on the site but the engineer. 'You're nearly finished, then, laddie?' he asked, in that cultured English voice that is so pleasant to the ear.

'Yes, unfortunately, I am,' I replied.

'Yes, that's the sad part: having to let you go. You're a good brickie. Have you anything lined up?' he asked.

'No, I'm afraid not.'

He looked at me intently before asking, 'Do you know anything about boilers?'

When one becomes proficient in a skill like laying out complicated brick jobs, one assumes a certain degree of assurance and confidence; also, one ceases to be unduly worried about the next job or about any problems that might arise. As a matter of fact, the opposite is often the case: as a young journeyman, I derived a certain quirky pleasure from anticipating what types of new jobs lay ahead. So, when the engineer asked me if I knew anything about boilers, my whole being cried out, 'No, no'; but the thought of a year or two's constant work with no wet time, and of how that could help my wife and young family, made me stammer out the lie.

'I know a little about them,' I half-whispered, unconsciously expecting someone to shout out, 'You know F-all about them!'

'What types of boilers are you familiar with?'

'Wilson and Lancashire boilers,' I muttered.

'That's a bit of luck; that's the two types we have.'

I was too weak at the knees to answer, so he continued speaking. 'Report to Jimmy Garland in the boiler-house Monday morning, and bring an old boiler suit with you.'

It was a very tired and rather distraught bricklayer who appeared in Killeen boiler-house on Monday morning. I had spent a very exhausting weekend trying to examine the logic of what I had done, for I had basically misrepresented myself as a tradesman. This kept needling me. From a very young age, Johnny and Brendan and I had had it drummed into us by our father that bricklaying was one of the oldest crafts known to man, and that any brickwork, no matter what form it takes, is one of the most enduring products of man. It therefore was incumbent on all who followed the craft to do everything in their power to emulate, or at least to try and imitate, that fine work carried out by our forebears. As my father would always say, 'We owe it to them that's gone before us to try to do as good work as they did.' I knew, from hearing brickies talking over the years, that boiler work was a very specialised type of work. On the other hand there was the chance that it would not only broaden my craft knowledge, but also result in me getting a year or two of steady work with the added bonus of regular holidays and no wet time.

'Are you all ready, laddie?' The engineer's voice cut in on my thoughts.

'Yes – yes, I think so,' I stammered.

'Well, as you can see, we have the Lancashire standing

down, so you and Jim Garland will be stripping it down completely. Then, when Tommy and I have examined it, you'll be re-bricking it. Any questions?'

'No, it looks straightforward enough,' I replied. I was hoping that he wouldn't ask me to get inside the boiler; this huge piece of metal reminded me of an old-fashioned railway engine without wheels – I hadn't a clue how one even entered it. Just then Jimmy Garland himself appeared, closely followed by his mate Jim McEvoy.

'You're all set, then, Billsyer?' he asked. Then, winking at me, he whispered, 'Go down behind the boiler, strip off everything but your underpants, then put on your old boiler suit – you did bring one?'

I nodded, and did as I was told. When I returned, Jim introduced me to Tommy Sherlock, a fitter in his late twenties. I soon found out that the boiler-house was the real hub or source of energy for the mill, and that Tommy was the young genius who kept those home fires burning. I also found out that between Jim and Tommy there was a special bond of a kind that seldom exists between men. Their friendship was based on each other's great knowledge of boiler-work; their combined knowledge was vast, and I deemed myself bloody lucky to be the beneficiary of such a legacy.

'Now, the boiler is only down a couple of days,' Jim said, addressing both our mates, 'so you two will need plenty of wet sacks. As we hand the dry ones out, you make sure you keep us supplied with very wet ones. Also, one of you stay in front of the boiler door at all times, in case we need you in a hurry.'

'But can we not leave it open?' I inquired.

'No, because if we did we'd be blown out of it with the fans. No, the door has to stay shut, so the man outside standing at the door is our only contact with the outside in case anything goes wrong.'

'What tools do I need to bring in with me?' I asked, looking at Jimmy as he placed a pad over his nose and mouth.

'Only your cold chisel and heavy hammer,' he answered, his voice muffled. 'The lads will hand us in anything else we want.'

He took up one of the soaking sacks lying on the floor and, bending down, opened a very small door at the base of the boiler – it could not have been more then eighteen inches square. Placing the wet sack at the base of this tiny opening, Jimmy bent down and disappeared inside. My entrance was more restrained: getting down on my hands and knees, I glanced inside the boiler. It was lit by two large bulbs at the ends of two lengths of cable; the bulbs themselves were encased in grids made of a rubber substance similar to what ice-hockey goalkeepers wear for protection.

My first impression on entering the interior of the boiler was of the terrible heat coming, not just from the hot brickwork that lined the side walls, but also from the floor. Our wet sacks, which we placed on the floor of the boiler so that it would not burn us, dried within minutes; replacing them was an almost continual chore. The primitive lighting cast great shadows, giving the interior of the large boiler an eerie, ghostly look. I watched Jimmy Garland remove the old brickwork with his hammer and chisel and followed suit, stopping every so often to drink from the jug of cold water that the two lads outside kept giving us. When we had accumulated a lot of old bricks on the floor around us, Jimmy beckoned to me to stand back; then he literally threw the bricks out through the small opening, and the lads outside removed them out of harm's way.

This type of work continued for about three days, until we had the Lancashire boiler stripped down to the bare metal. Then we rested, while Tommy Sherlock and his crew of fitters and electricians descended upon the heap of still-hot metal, checking everything and replacing anything that needed to be replaced. I helped Jimmy Garland check on the new fire-bricks that had arrived, along with the many tins of fire-clay used to joint the bricks.

'I always thought that fire-clay was black,' I said.

'It was, and still is,' was Jimmy's reply. 'But this is new stuff called Peruma, and you spread it on the brick like butter. It makes a real tight joint, just like a fish's arse.'

'A fish's arse?'

'Aye – and that's watertight,' said Jim without a smile.

The new stuff, as Jimmy called, it was indeed great stuff. You buttered it on the brick you were about to lay; then, having lined the exposed walls of the boiler with sheets of asbestos, you drove the brick home with your brick-hammer, following the curve of the boiler wall at all times so as not to form a vacuum where air could remain and cause a blow-back.

I soon found that one dispensed with the usual plumbing and only used one's small boat level and rule. I enjoyed forming the different arches, especially the ringed arch. This type of arch is usually used where appearance is of minor importance but the strength of the arch is all-important – in sewers and bridge-work, for example – as one can create two or more rings for added strength.

When we finished for the day, we were allowed a two-hour cooling-off and washing-up period. This amounted to twelve hours' overtime a week – a godsend. On the building sites, overtime was always referred to as 'OT', and in those days it was as scarce as hen's teeth. But in Killeen Paper Mill it was known as 'crust'; and among the fitters, the electricians and most of the building workers, every job that was coming up was judged by the amount of crust that was expected. At first I, coming off the building sites – where one felt lucky to have a job, even with wet time thrown in – could not relate to this 'greed', as I saw it; but I have to say that, before the first year was out, I was also there with my hand held up high when the magic word 'crust' was mentioned.

The only drawback to our 'cooling-off' time was the lack of proper washing-up facilities. This being the early 50s, it was, it seemed, acceptable both to unions and to nearly all managements of industrial plants that we should wash the soot off our bodies with industrial soap. That is, until one evening when we were sitting outside the boiler-house, very exhausted after completing the re-bricking of the boiler. Suddenly Jimmy spotted the resident nurse, who was a permanent fixture in the mill and who did some great work using her considerable skills when accidents and other emergencies took place.

'Nurse, can I have a word?' Jim's tone was conciliatory.

'Yes, certainly; that's what I'm here for.'

Jim stood up. His face and body, like mine, were as black as the proverbial ace of spades. 'Can we have some soap to wash ourselves with, please?'

'As far as I know there's plenty of industrial soap in stock, but I'll check to make sure,' she answered.

As the nurse started to walk away, Jimmy's tone changed. 'I don't want that bloody soap – I want the nine-out-of-ten soap!'

The nurse looked slightly stunned. 'Nine out of ten? What ever do you mean?' she asked.

'I mean what the nine out of ten film stars use!' shouted Jimmy. Turning to me, he nodded in the nurse's direction. 'You explain to her, Billsyer.'

I had a flash of inspiration. 'You mean you want Nurse to arrange for us to have a bar of Lux soap?'

He gave me a look that went right through me. 'Isn't that what I've been sayin' all the time?'

The nurse smiled a broad smile and disappeared, only to reappear a few minutes later carrying a bar of Lux soap. It was forevermore known in the mill as 'the nine-out-of-ten'.

Another feature of the mill that attracted me was the reading material that came in as waste. A lot of magazine publishers discarded copies that were not up to standard, and they would end up in what we called 'the broke'. The result was that, after reading our copies of the *Reader's Digest*, a small group of us would try to improve our English by using the special 'word of the month' in our conversations with one another.

I quickly learned that the production of paper was the prime objective and that everything else, no matter what you thought, followed way behind. Even so, it took a considerable time before I got used to the fact that you could have a board full of mortar and be at a critical stage of some building job, yet when you got the word to report to the boiler-house you were expected to report immediately. 'Production, production, production,' was the cry.

There was a large maintenance group employed by the mill. As well as fitters, electricians and wheelwrights, there were two carpenters, two painters, and Garland and myself as the two brickies, and each tradesman had his own mate. Also, there were about ten building workers. They always worked in two separate groups, each group or gang having its own ganger and its own place to eat; the unwritten law seemed to be, 'Never the twain shall meet.'

And, of course, among these men were characters whom God, in his few moments of divilment, created for his own and our amusement. One of these was a man they called 'the Thick' – because he was anything but thick. Bestowing on certain people names that are in complete opposition to their real characters is a very Irish habit! For example, the mill's engineer, who spoke with a very distinctive upper-class English accent, was called 'Din-Joe' – a name derived from an old radio-show character who spoke in a broad West Cork accent.

One Friday morning, the Thick arrived into work wearing beautiful corduroy trousers that were so new they shouldn't have been taken away from their mother. His ganger was delighted; he whispered to me – rather boastfully, I thought – 'It adds a touch of class to our squad.' All day long, as the word spread, men came from all over the mill to view these brown corduroy pants. This was unknown to the wearer, who went about his work with his usual lack of zeal, completely unaware that he was distracting his fellow workers – whose taste, judging by some of the awful clobber they were inclined to wear, was crude.

The following Monday morning, someone discovered that the Thick wasn't wearing his new corduroys; he was back in his old overalls with the large ventilation holes covered by patches of various colourful materials. It seemed to be a case of rags to riches in reverse. His ganger was dumbfounded and selected Charlie, one of the lads, to ask the Thick what had happened to the lovely corduroy trousers.

The Thick scratched his head and, looking straight at Charlie, whispered, 'You don't want to know.' But Charlie persisted in wanting to know what had happened to the trousers.

'Well,' said the Thick, 'it must have been that last pint of stout I had last night, but as I threw my leg over the oul' bike this morning I felt a terrible ball of wind buildin' up in me stomach. Having passed that, I suddenly realised that I had wet meself; and then, before I could get off the bicycle, I found I had shit in them as well.'

Charlie, being a horsy man, looked at the Thick and said, 'You got up a treble, then?'

'You could say that, Charlie,' the Thick replied. 'But the bike stank to high heaven – I had to have it put down.'

After the freedom of working on building sites, I found working in a place like Killeen Paper Mill very restrictive. For instance, once we had clocked in, we couldn't go outside the mill without permission; there was no smoking, except in the toilets; and, if we in the building section needed any water for building purposes, we had to draw it from the river. But one cold winter's morning the Thick, having been directed by his ganger to take the dumper down to the river and fill it up with water, opted instead to draw the water from the many hydrants that were situated around the mill – an offence punishable by instant dismissal. As he was filling up the dumper, who should come around the corner but the engineer.

'What are you doing, laddie?' enquired the engineer.

'Filling the dumper up with water, sir,' answered the Thick. I was expecting the engineer to inform him that he was sacked.

'Now, you know the rules, laddie: only river water to be used on all projects connected with the building sector. So your explanation for using hydrant water better be good.'

The Thick looked at the hydrant, then at the engineer, then back at the hydrant again.

'I'm waiting, laddie,' said the engineer, rubbing his hands together.

'Well, I tried the river water in the carburettor, sir, but I found it very sluggish.'

The engineer, who had been in the Royal Navy for a number of years and had a vast knowledge and experience of engineering, must have heard some way-out excuses in his time; but he just smiled and said softly, 'As long as you have an answer, laddie, as long as you have an answer.' Then he walked away.

My first couple of years of working in the mill passed quickly, and, apart from the heat and the dirt of the boilers, they were pleasant years. I was earning a constant wage every week and the odd bit of overtime thrown in, plus a bonus at Christmastime. Once the autumn days started to close in on us, this bonus, which was an extra week's wages, became the sole topic of conversation – spurred on, no doubt, by the usual rumour-spreaders who gloried in telling you that they had heard from a very reliable source in the head office that there were to be no bonuses that year. All kinds of reasons were given: the state of the world markets, the drop in production, the unfair demands of the many unions representing the various workers employed in the mill... But, of course, as reliable as old Santa, the bonus always appeared in the pay packet the week before Christmas. In that world of big business, it was nice to know that the people at the top were willing to share a little of the profits with us, and I take this opportunity to thank them, for it helped to bring Santa into our home. In all my years of working hard for builders, I don't remember many of them handing out an extra week's wages to their workers at Christmastime.

After my first year in the mill, Jimmy Garland and I decided to organise a Christmas stag party. The men who wanted to come could give us a half-crown a week from about the start of October; that would entitle them to a dinner, a few drinks and a taxi home. Every week, the men who were coming handed me their half-crowns as soon as they were paid – all except one, who, after a few weeks, stopped giving me any money. Well, the night of the party, who should turn up at the hotel but our local Scrooge! I had to prevail upon the rest of the lads to let this fellow in, for I didn't want any trouble. Later, after paying out all our expenses, Jimmy and I discovered that we had a surplus of money, so we decided to divide it among the men who had paid into the fund. The next Monday morning, we passed the word around the mill for the men to come and collect their rebate. I could not believe it when our local Scrooge turned up and demanded his share. As my father used to say, 'It's a queer world, inhabited by queerer people.'

But I'm glad to say that the Killeen Christmas Party became an annual event and grew with the years. I have very fond memories of the songs, the music, and above all the friendships that were copper-fastened at these events. For you can work with a man day in and day out, but I believe that until you share food and drink in a spirit of conviviality with another person, you can never really and truly know him – and to know someone is to trust, or not trust, him.

The Secret of Manhood

The unfeeling of this earth
Snub you for being poor
And make you feel ashamed.
They judge you on the way you speak
Not how you play the game.
These fools, these fools
Will never learn
What makes a man a man;
These fools, these fools
Will never learn
A man is born a man.

CHAPTER 16

The Death of My Father

One August morning in 1956, my world was turned upside down.

'I'm sorry to have to tell you this,' the engineer said to me, 'but your father has fallen off a scaffolding. He is seriously ill in the Mater Hospital. Your sister rang up on behalf of your mother; she's on the phone now – you can pick it up in my office. I think she would like you to go to the hospital as soon as possible. So off you go; I'll attend to things here.'

These words pierced not just my heart, but my brain as well; for, as the sailor's nearest and dearest dread the words 'lost at sea', so the family of the building worker dread those words, 'fall from a scaffold'. There is an old saying in the building trade that any kind of fall does the fallen no good.

When I arrived at the Mater Hospital, I found out that my father was critically ill, but the real extent of his injuries was still not clear, as the doctors had not completed their examination of him. Later that night, we were informed by a senior surgeon that my father had broken his back. There was a good chance that he might walk again, but he would never work again.

It was heartbreaking to see the Da just lying there – this man who, when we were small, used to put Johnny and me on his bicycle and cycle up to Baldonnell Aerodrome, a distance of over six miles each way, just because we two youngsters loved to see the aeroplanes landing and taking off; all this after a hard day's work. He and my mother were a real married couple: they enjoyed each other's company, and they shared everything – household chores, shopping expeditions into the city for clothes, and that very important visit every year to old Santa. And most years, if the Da got a few nixers, the family would benefit from a holiday by the sea. He was the one you always tried to sit nearest to when the noise of the thunder was loud and frightening and those terrible flashes of lightning lit up the room; when, for that very brief moment, you could see, with your fanciful young eyes, the bushes outside taking on an evil animal form that seemed to hurl itself against the glass of the window. It was then he'd wink at you, hug you and whisper, 'It'll be all right, son.' And it always was. That was his legacy to us, this very dependable person who seemed to fear nothing, who stood like a rock between us and the world.

Yet there was a boyishness in him that bubbled to the surface now and then. I remember well the evening he brought Johnny and myself to see Gene Autry on stage in the Theatre Royal. There was a short film on first, showing Gene saying good-bye to his pal Smiley as he left for Ireland, then crossing rivers and fighting hordes of red Indians. Suddenly there was a roll of drums, and who should come riding out onto the stage, on the back of his famous horse Champion, but Gene Autry himself! That was the cue for the youthful audience to rise as one, cheering the young singing cowboy. I can still see my father, up on his feet, cheering with the rest of us.

Later, as we got older, he was the person you went to, to explain yourself, if Mother and you had had a row over something or other. You had to listen to what he had to say, and you usually agreed, however reluctantly, to his solution. That, I think, was the measure of the man.

We were delighted to see that the surgeon was right: the Da

did make a remarkable recovery, and in a few months he was able to walk, with the aid of a steel corset that helped strengthen his back. Then disaster struck again.

He and my mother, who were both great theatre-goers, had been at the Abbey Theatre one Saturday night, and as usual I arrived at the house the following Sunday morning with Geraldine, my eldest little girl, to share two bottles of stout with the Da and to be told the details of the play they had seen. He was in great form – then, suddenly, he seemed unwell. He had suffered a stroke.

Back in hospital, we discovered that he had lost the use of one side of his body. But, thanks be to God, he still had his other faculties: he could speak and think fairly rationally. For instance, he would not allow the barber in the hospital to shave him – as he said, 'That man might have just shaved someone down in the dead-house' – so Brendan, my younger brother (Johnny, the oldest brother, had got married and emigrated to Australia in 1950), and I used to go in and shave him every night with the help and co-operation of the nursing staff. On 27 November, his birthday, I bought him a pair of socks; on my birthday, which was three days later, he suggested to my mother that she put the new socks into another bag and give them to me. 'Sure he'll never know the difference,' were the Da's words.

He was to be released from hospital on a Sunday morning, but on the Saturday night we got a call from the hospital to say that he wasn't too well. I went over to see him. The doctor told me that he had had an egg for his tea, and that it could have upset him. I asked him if my father would still be coming home the next day.

'Yes, of course,' said he. 'You can go in to him now, but don't stay too long; I want him to rest.'

The Da seemed very surprised to see me. 'What are you doing here at this hour?' he asked.

I told him I was out having a drink for my birthday, and he seemed to believe me. Then he said, 'Son, if anything happens to me, I want you to look after things; but I also want you to make sure that, when you're putting it in the papers, you don't forget to say, "Late of the Ancient Guild of Incorporated Brick and Stonelayers, 49 Cuffe Street".'

I looked at him, not exactly hearing what he was saying, but knowing deep down in my gut that he was saying it. 'Hey, Da,' I remember saying, 'you must have got more than an egg for your tea to be talking foolish like that.'

Just then the nurse came in and said it would be better not to tire out him out, as he needed rest. As I said good-bye, my father did something he had very seldom done before – he shook my hand. The time was about ten o'clock.

At twelve midnight, we got a call from the hospital to say that Mr French had just died. Going into the hospital early next morning, Brendan and I went up to his ward to ask the man in the next bed to the Da's what had happened, as he had died so soon after I had been with him.

'Did he say anything after I left?' I enquired.

'No,' said the man. 'After you left, your father turned his face to the wall and I could hear him crying softly to himself; then he just stopped and died very quietly.'

For him to die on his own – after rearing eight of us, and at only fifty-six years of age – was, in my opinion, a terrible obscenity.

In the mid-1950s, while the rest of Europe experienced a period of economic growth and rising living standards, Ireland plunged deeper into a recession. We who were very active in the trade union movement at that time could not understand how, on the continent of Europe, real national incomes rose by 40 per cent, and even in Britain incomes rose by 21 per cent, whereas here in Ireland the rise was only 8 per cent. This huge gap between English and Irish wages led to mass emigration. It was estimated that, between 1951 and 1956, over two hundred thousand people left our shores to seek, not just a better life, but a living for themselves and their families. This terrible drain on the nation, and the pain of individual families whose fathers, sons, and daughters were leaving, was impossible to calculate. My own sister Margaret and my brother Brendan were among those who had to go at that time.

Then, just when one thought things could not get any worse, they did. Along came the Suez crisis, and the economic situation worsened greatly when petrol was rationed. A very tough budget in the same year did little to improve the people's outlook. With all the doom and gloom around, it was inevitable that the building trade would grind to a halt, which it did in the autumn of 1956. The number of people unemployed rose to its peak in 1957, with over 78,000 idle. Many of these people were living on a small unemployment benefit, which lasted for only six months; after that, unemployed workers had to submit to a belittling means test that might, if they were lucky, give them a mere pittance.

In an attempt to come to grips with the critical economic situation, the coalition government set up a committee with representatives from the industrial and trade union movements, under the direction of Dr T.K. Whitaker. This committee produced a programme for economic expansion, which was the very start of the long way back for us as a nation. Then, in 1957, we joined the International Monetary Fund. That was a very big step: up to that time, all our payments to other countries had been made in British currency.

When the Fianna Fáil government was returned to power in 1957, de Valera stepped down soon afterwards. The newly elected Taoiseach, Sean Lemass, was nearly sixty years of age at the time, but he proved to be the right man for the job. There was a stir in the air, a feeling of something awakening. New industrial firms were being attracted to Ireland, new factories were springing up everywhere; and we in Killeen Paper Mill benefited from this new unexpected boom, with the mill's management embarking on a fairly comprehensive programme of building. We built extensions to three of the machine rooms, and a large canteen for the workers. In between all this new work, Jim Garland and I still had to service and maintain the old boilers. Of course, all this building activity brought in a regular wage plus a fair sprinkling of crust, for which my wife and I, and our expanding family, were very grateful.

The General Manager of Killeen Paper Mill, Mr Munford, an Englishman by birth, lived in a large old house at the rear of the mill. One day, as I was standing looking up at the new canteen we were building, his booming voice cut across my thoughts.

'Have you nothing to do, Bip?' he inquired – he called everyone 'Bip'.

'I have, Mr Munford,' I answered. 'At the moment I'm trying to figure out the best way to knock down that old wall there.'

'Which wall?'

'That old stone wall there. It's right in the way of the thirteen-and-a-half-inch wall that will form the back of the new canteen,' I replied, pointing out a large black section of stone wall covered with moss and ivy. I was delighted that I had an answer for him, for he was a fair but hard taskmaster.

He looked hard at me and shouted, in a voice that made me squirm with embarrassment – especially as some of the other building workers were there – 'Have you no soul, man?'

'I don't know what you mean, Mr Munford,' I stammered.

'Well, let me tell you, then,' he said. 'That old wall, as you call it, was part of this mill long, long before you and I were ever heard of. That is part of our heritage – and you want to knock it down. Let me tell you something, Bip: you'll go before that wall does. Do I make myself clear?'

'But, Mr Munford,' I protested – noting the smug smiles on the faces of the other building workers, who were delighted that they were not the ones in the firing line – 'it clearly says here on the drawing that the old wall is to be demolished.'

With one wave of his hand he dismissed the drawing. 'I'm not interested in drawings, I'm interested in history. And so should you be – even more than me, because it's your own country.'

After he left, Jim Brophy and I climbed to the top of the old wall, where we discovered a bird's nest with three tiny open mouths inside, while their poor mother tried to imitate the miracle of the loaves and fishes by dividing the small worm in her mouth into three parts. As Paddy Pearse once wrote, 'The world is hard on mothers.'

After a discussion between management and Jimmy O'Callaghan, it was decided to incorporate that section of the old mill wall into the new wall of the canteen. There were also explicit orders from Mr Munford himself that nothing was to be done that would upset the birds' nest or its occupants.

One morning shortly afterwards, there seemed to be a lot of chattering coming from the nest. Thinking that maybe a cat or rat was the reason for all the noise, I climbed up onto the top of the old wall, and witnessed something that has stayed with me all through the years.

It was obvious from the fluttering of the two larger birds that the time had come for the three wee ones to fly the nest. After a while, as we watched, two of the younger birds climbed onto the edge of the nest and flew away. Then I realised the chattering came from the one remaining little bird, who refused to leave his nice warm bed. But, unfortunately for him, old Mother Nature had to take her course. Bending down, the parents of the wee bird took one of his wings in each of their beaks and, flying high, just dropped him like a stone. As we watched, his tiny wings fluttered and he too started to fly. Although we waited and waited, none of the birds ever came back to the nest.

When we had the main walls completed, the steel arrived for the roof. Steel-erecting is carried out by specialists, who are called spidermen because of their agility and their ability to work at very dangerous heights. It tends to be a family job, where the skills are often passed from father to son. It's a tough job, and the men working at it have to be equal to the task.

In those days of the early 60s, we were not supplied with protective headgear, and one day, as Jim Garland and I were laying out the internal walls, a cold rivet fell near me. Looking up, I shouted, 'Hey, be careful up there!'

A voice from above answered back, 'Ah, go and get stuffed, yeh mouth yeh.'

Losing my temper, I shouted back, 'I dare you to repeat those remarks down here.'

Unfortunately, the spiderman took the dare. In five seconds flat he had hopped down to the ground; he ran at me, swinging a heavy wrench in his hand. At this stage, Providence thankfully intervened, in the shape of Jimmy Garland. Pushing me aside, Jimmy raised his trowel and aimed it right between the eyes of the spiderman; seeing it coming, he turned his head, only to catch the full force of Garland's trowel on the side of his face.

As his hands covered the wound and the blood poured out over them, the spiderman kept shouting, 'Oh, me poor listener is gone – me poor listener is gone!' He was referring to his left ear, which was badly cut. Even at the time, I thought it very funny that a man so deep in pain would use the pure inner-city lingo to express his fear about losing his ear.

Later, after the nurse had stopped the flow of blood and

cleaned up the wound, the bandaged spiderman became good friends with Jimmy and me. Such is the strange comradeship among building workers.

A bricklayer, unlike a carpenter, very seldom concerns himself with plans or the taking of levels. Usually he is given a sketch showing the sizes of the door and window openings and their positions in relation to the rest of the building. So our knowledge of the detailed reading of maps and the taking of levels from benchmarks is very often sketchy, to say the least. I was very lucky to encounter Jimmy Callaghan, a fine draughtsman who was willing to work closely with us. I said to him, 'We know the building game, and you know all about map-reading and level-taking, so let's share our knowledge.' This we did, and I want to thank him for all that knowledge he imparted to me and to Jim Garland. Little did I know then, as I studied the various maps with their distinctive contours and markings and learned how to use the theodolite efficiently enough to measure different angles when laying out a new building or extension, that all this knowledge would be invaluable to me one day.

Is being in the right place at the right time just a matter of luck? Or is it, as the theologians like to say, part of a definite plan? And, if so, why? Why should a God bother about little oul' me, when there are millions of poor people in this world down on their knees crying out for help? Yet I'm convinced that He took that trouble. For a person who tied himself to a trade that, by its very nature, is vulnerable to the ever-changing weather patterns and to the constant cycles of work and no work, I seem, against all the odds, to have led a charmed life, never having been idle until the day I retired. Now, after more than seventy years on this earth, I firmly believe that, if you are born with all the faculties required to make a success of whatever field you choose to work in, you are given an extra something that allows you to see and to seize the opportunities that present themselves from time to time. I also believe that, because this extra something is indefinable in the world in which we live, it must come from a spiritual power outside the body. Theologians, I suppose, would call it spiritual intervention. But, whatever it's called, I am convinced that it must stem from a greater Power.

I am also convinced that, no matter how many times it's said or how many books are written on the subject, we do not learn from other people's mistakes. Also, added years do not necessarily endow one with earth-shattering or brain-boggling knowledge. I always remember hearing, on a radio show, Somerset Maugham's answer to the question, 'Mr Maugham, you have lived well into your ninetieth year. What profound discovery have you made, after living all those years, that you feel you could pass on to future generations?' Somerset Maugham's reply was, 'If you get a chance to go to the toilet, take it.'

I once met an old man coming out of a doctor's surgery; he was smiling in a delightful way. I said, 'You look as if you're after getting very good news.'

'Yes, I am,' he said, still smiling. 'I said to the doctor that there must be something wrong with my kidneys, as I hadn't passed water in the last three days.'

'And what did he say?' I asked.

'He said, "What age are you?" I said I was ninety-two. And do you know what he said to me?' the old man asked.

'No.'

'He said, "Ah, sure, you've pissed enough."'

And who knows? Maybe he had.

CHAPTER 17

Milking the Shovel

One day, like all building stories, my time at Killeen Paper Mill came to an end. Management decided that enough building had been completed to fulfil their needs. So, keeping only the necessary maintenance staff, like Jimmy Garland for the boilers, they made most of us redundant.

After six years of constant work, I found it a great shock to my system to be sacked. Unfortunately for us, in those days there was no such thing as redundancy money. So, having collected the money due to me at the front office, I threw my leg over my old bike and, without looking back, cycled home with my tools and the bad news.

The next morning, a Saturday, I cycled down to Cuffetown, as we brickies called the Bricklayers' Hall. There I met with the union secretary, Frank O'Connor. After I explained my tale of woe, Frank told me that Cooney the builder was building an extension to a factory at the back of the quays and was looking for a bricklayer to lay out the new building.

I immediately went over to the site, which was just off Smithfield, and met Eddie Steel, the general foreman. He showed me the plans and asked me if I could start work the following Monday morning. My answer was, 'Could a cat drink milk?'

Although I was, like the rest of the lads on the site, on wet time when it rained, it was a happy job. Eddie and I worked closely together. A carpenter by trade, he had a vast knowledge both of building and of men.

Yet, for all his knowledge, he – like the rest of us – was completely taken in one day, when a man wearing a dark suit that had seen better days and happier nights appeared on the site.

'Kind sir, may I speak to you?' said this man in a voice that would not have been out of place in Oxford or Trinity.

'Yes, of course,' replied Eddie. 'What is it you want?'

'A job, sir,' replied your man, standing to attention army-style.

'A job – doing what?' asked a perplexed Eddie.

'Anything. I have fallen on bad times, sir, so I'll take anything you have to offer in the way of honest toil.'

'What experience have you?' inquired Eddie, glancing at me with complete puzzlement on his face.

'You name it, sir. I've been a soldier, a sailor and a priest, among other things.'

'I can only offer you labouring work,' said Eddie.

'Sir, once it's honest toil, the Lord will bless it.'

The upshot of it was that Eddie hired the Professor, as he was soon dubbed. For the first few days, this strange man performed any and every job given to him, no matter how menial the task, and was very courteous to all at all times. But after the first week, our professor friend began to disappear when some dirty job needed to be done; and even when on the job, he was inclined to 'milk the shovel' – as they say in the building game about a person who, rather than using the shovel as per the instructions on the label, simply places it under one arm and uses it as a crutch for the bewildered.

One morning, Eddie and I went to the back of the old factory to check on some measurements and spotted the Professor spread out on a couple of dirty old sacks, half-asleep.

'What in the name of Christ are you doing there?' Eddie's voice was loud and harsh.

If the Professor was startled, he didn't let it show. 'I'm just resting,' said he in a bored voice.

'Resting – did he say resting?' demanded Eddie, looking at me in complete disbelief.

'I think that's what he said,' I muttered, trying to hide the grin on my face. 'Why are you resting at this hour of the morning?' I asked the Professor.

'Well, Billy, when I was being assessed for the priesthood, many years ago, they told me that one of the main attributes God had seen fit to give me was laziness. And, being a born-again Christian, I like to think that – for His sake – I should use His gift to the full.'

'Born-again Christian, are yeh?' Eddie's voice was rising. 'When I'm finished with yeh, you'll wish you'd never been born. In other words, as the bishop said to the canon, you're fired!'

The Professor left us rather hurriedly, without even the benefit of a blessing.

One morning, after the job was laid out up to damp-course level, a few more brickies arrived from other sites to 'get it up or go to jail', as we say in the building game. Among them I was delighted to see Miley Byrne, a real Dublin character, and the brothers Paddy and Michael Whelan. These three had just come back from Kerry, where they had been building a church in the heart of the old county. Paddy and Michael, because of their old republican connections, had been received like royalty in the Kingdom, whereas Miley had been like a fish out of water. And, like all journeymen, they had tales to tell.

Michael was telling us about the digs they had been in, and how nice the landlady had been, when Miley interrupted him with, 'Feckin' oul' wan – she was always hovering over yeh when you were trying to eat something.'

'She was good to you,' Paddy said.

'What do you mean, good to me? How?'

'First thing in the morning when you came down to breakfast, she was over to you to ask how you like your eggs, soft or hard. And all you could say was, "Why, is it you or the hens that's doing the laying?" She was a nice lady, and I think she had a soft spot for you, Miley,' said Paddy, winking at the rest of us.

But Miley would have none of it. 'Well, it's a pity she didn't put that soft spot in the centre of her eggs – like bullets, they were. A man would be farting all day after eating one of them. I think her poor oul' hens were shell-shocked. I still say you can't beat the Dublin mot for cooking.' Miley put a cigarette in his mouth and lit it with a burning stick taken from the open fire.

'Where were the digs in relation to the church job?' I asked.

'About three miles away,' said Paddy. 'And every day, as we drove along the narrow roads, we had to pass this old cottage. Outside this cottage, morning and night, sat an oul' fella in a big old armchair, and in the centre of the dirt road opposite him lay this dog – a big oul' mutt, he was, just lying there. The driver of our van used to have to drive round him. So one day, being a dog lover, I told the driver to pull up; and when he did, I said to the old man, "Do you realise that dog of yours is going to be killed out there on the road some day?"'

'And what did he say?' I asked.

'First he took the pipe out of his mouth,' replied Paddy, 'and then, fixing his eyes on me, he said, "Aye, I wouldn't be at all surprised, sir. His poor father was killed in the very same spot." Then, putting the pipe back in his mouth, he went back to doing nothing.'

Michael, laughing, said to his older brother, 'It was the best "F off" you ever got in Kerry.' And Paddy agreed.

'Tell them about your man dying and Miley and the widow,' said Paddy to his brother.

'Oh, that was funny – well, not so funny for the poor divil that died,' said Michael. 'But funny all the same. You see, one of the old local men who was working on the church with us wasn't feeling too well; and one evening, after going home, he took a turn for the worse and just died. It was all rather sudden. When we finished up the next day, the three of us went over to your man's house to pay our respects.'

'I don't know why we did – sure, we hardly knew the fella,' muttered Miley.

'Well, you have to be respectful, don't you?' demanded Paddy. We all nodded in agreement.

'Well,' Michael continued, 'over we go to the widow, surrounded as she was by all the old neighbours, and we lined up to pay our respects. Then Miley here nudges me. "What will I say?" says he. I told him, "Just say you're very sorry to hear her husband has died, and then pass on into the other room where the corpse is laid out."'

'And that's precisely what I did, isn't it?' growled Miley, getting the last drag out of his cigarette.

'Yes, it is, Miley, up to a point. But when the widow told you her husband had done his duty ten minutes before he died, she meant that he had received the last rites – *not* that he had had sex; and you saying to the poor new widow, "Sure, that was probably what killed him," didn't help!'

One day I was working inside the entrance to the site when a man appeared with a parcel under his arm. He looked hard at me and whispered, 'Do you want to buy a new pair of boots?'

I looked at his shifty stance and immediately said, 'No.'

Glancing around, he placed the brown-paper parcel on top of a barrel near me. 'I'll leave them there with you – you might change your mind. They're a brand-new pair, and I'll give them to you for three quid.' And he walked away.

All day long the parcel lay there untouched, until, at about four o'clock, one of the lads said to me, 'What's in the parcel?' When I told him, he opened the parcel and took out a new pair of shiny black boots. He bent down and removed his own dirty, worn-out boots, and proceeded to put on the new pair. After walking up and down like one of those models one sees on the telly, he bowed to us before putting his old crapped-out boots into the parcel and leaving it back on the same barrel.

Later, as we were packing up for the day, our friend the salesman appeared. 'Well,' he said to me, still furtively looking around him, 'do yeh want the boots or not?'

I, speechless, shook my head. Turning to the other lads nearby, the salesman asked the same question – but it was a bit more personal: 'Do any of you bloody bogmen want a pair of new boots?'

The lad who had taken the boots – and who came from Edenderry, near the Bog of Allen – called out, 'No, we don't want your boots, and furthermore I resent you calling us bogmen! Now, if you're not off this site in ten seconds, I'm going to give you a kick in the arse with *my* new boots.' And the lad had the cheek to show the poor salesman his own shiny new boots.

The unsuccessful salesman quickly grabbed his brown parcel and disappeared. And – strange but true – he never appeared on our site again.

Shortly afterwards, when the job was near completion, I was shifted out to Foxrock to help build bungalows. While working on the bungalows I got to know Mr Cooney personally, and I found him to be a real gentleman, intelligent and well read, with a very strong Christian belief in morality.

This was a pleasant surprise for me, for I had met one or two builders who would never qualify for the Brain of the Year; their one aim in life was to keep from spending money. I remember one builder who went by the name of Hoppy, because he had a bad leg. Then, one day, one of the lads on his site discovered that in the morning the builder hopped on his right leg; after lunch he hopped on his left leg.

'Why would he do that?' someone inquired.

'Because he's so bloody mean he doesn't want to wear out his shoes too soon. This way he gets twice as much wear out of them.' A funny story – maybe!

Mr Cooney and I found a lot of common ground, due to the fact that I had been studying Social Ethics under the Jesuits in Milltown. Our informal talks ranged over a wide area, covering topics such as the nature of moral principles and the responsibility of the individual in both private and public life.

I remember being very upset that our private conversations were frowned on by a good few of my fellow workers, simply because I was, as they saw it, fraternising with the enemy. Old habits die hard, especially in the workplace. We had just left the terrible 50s, years of unemployment and emigration that had drained away our nation's precious blood. We were entering the swinging 60s – the decade of enlightenment, we were told; but, in Ireland, a 'them and us' attitude still prevailed among all too many workers and employers.

When my work at the bungalows was finished, I was transferred to a large new site at the Philips factory in Clonskeagh. As I was earning an extra threepence a hour, Mr Murphy, the site manager, gave me the job of laying out the roads. This was done by clearing the new ground, marking it out, and then laying and levelling large kerbstones in sand and cement to form the roads.

When the first section of the factory was completed, there was an official opening ceremony attended by the top brass from Holland. After the speeches, food and other pleasantries, they were given the tour that nearly always seems to be part of these affairs. I was down on my knees, levelling one of the kerbstones, when who should stop and chat to me but the managing director himself.

'How many of you are laying out the roads?' he asked.

'Three of us,' I replied, getting up off my knees.

'Good. And have you any problems?' he inquired.

'No, I don't think so,' I said. Then, to show him what we were doing, I added, 'As soon as we can get a bulldozer, we'll knock down that big old tree there, and then carry on to finish this road.'

'What tree?' he asked harshly.

'That one there,' I said, pointing to the large tree in front of us and wondering if all the good wine had dimmed the big man's view.

The managing director looked at me and repeated, almost word for word, what Mr Munford had said to me about the old wall in Killeen Paper Mill over a year before. The gist of it was that I would go before the tree would. Going back many years later, I found the tree standing where we had left it.

Strange: I had lived in this lovely green island of ours for nearly thirty-five years, and it had taken two foreign gentlemen, one English and the other Dutch, to show me its beauty in such a forceful way. It made me hang my head in shame at the way we, all of us, have allowed uncaring developers to rape our countryside. They say it's hard to define a mortal sin; but, in my opinion, closing our eyes to such destruction is a mortal sin.

CHAPTER 18

Across the Pond

A month or two later, when I was attending a committee meeting in Cuffetown, I heard that Thompson the builder was looking for a bricklayer to go to England to study new damp-proofing methods. I applied, and I soon had the pleasure of meeting Mr Thompson himself; I found him to be a proper gentleman. Shortly after the interview, I was accepted. I was to sail to England and take a six-week crash course. For me, it was another leg in the journey of a journeyman.

My reason for wanting to go to England was not, as some might suggest, to fly the nest. I wanted to try and build some kind of permanent future for my wife and young children – Geraldine, then aged six, William, aged four, and little Mary, aged two. Having had a taste of continuous employment in Killeen Paper Mills for six years, both my wife and I found it very upsetting not to be able to plan holidays, or even invest in new furniture, due to the lack of a constant wage.

With this in mind, I had inquired about a job in the Guinness Brewery that I had heard about through the grapevine; the brewery was looking for a brickie to service some boilers. I had spoken to the person concerned, and thought I was doing well until he asked me what age I was. 'Thirty-five,' said I, knowing that the person asking the question would never again see thirty-five except on the proverbial hall door. 'I'm sorry,' he said, 'I'm afraid you're too old.' Those words were still ringing in my ears as I threw my leg across my old bicycle and journeyed home. I suddenly felt old – and, worse still, I had nothing to show for it.

That was why, when the opportunity arose to study new damp-course methods, I seized it with both hands. It meant having to go to England for a while, but I didn't mind – especially when it was hinted that, if the new method took off here in Dublin, I could expect a permanent job.

As I left the North Wall on that boat bound for Liverpool, one rainy night in the autumn of '63, my mind was full of anticipation, coupled with fear of what lay beyond as I wondered if I would be able to grasp these newfangled ideas about damp-coursing – and, of course, great sorrow at leaving my young family for several long weeks. Then I thought of all the thousands of people, including my own brothers and sister, who had taken the same boat into the unknown waters of emigration. I was not being pushed, as they were, by successive governments' mishandling of the Irish economy. I was going for only a few weeks, and at the end of it there was the promise of a permanent job... There, again, was this obsession with having a constant wage to provide for my young family. Was that a good thing, or had I let it overrule everything else? Man is surely driven by strange winds.

When I arrived at Euston railway station, I stood like lost baggage waiting to be claimed. The people I was to meet had it all worked out: 'Tell Mr French to wear a large green hanky in his breast pocket.' That appeared to be a simple request, but it could only have come from somebody with no knowledge of Ireland at that time. My poor wife walked the streets of Dublin in search of a green hanky, but in vain: no green hanky could she buy or borrow. So I had to wait until I was claimed by the boss himself, Mr Flanagan – a big man, an Australian and bloody proud of it. After being in his company for an hour and having in that time drunk three or more whiskies, I even began to like Australia.

Over a meal, he explained to me the nature of the work. It fulfilled a real need: a lot of houses in the London area needed their damp-proof courses renewed to prevent rising damp. So Mr Flanagan had, after a lot of trial and error, invented this method where three bricklayers, working flat out, could insert a complete new damp-course in an average-sized house in just one week.

I was to work with two brothers from Scotland. One of them, having taken me home for a meal, agreed that it would be best if I took lodgings with him and his family. In that way he could fill me in on any questions I might have – for, as he said to me at the time, 'We don't talk on the job, we just bloody well work.' When they arrived at a house to be damp-proofed, the two brothers tossed a coin to determine who was to be the foreman; after that, no further discussion took place. The appointed foreman just directed you to your place, told you what to do and then got on with his own work.

Once you had determined the levels and the thickness of the outer wall, you were given a mechanical saw that allowed you to penetrate an inch beyond the centre of the wall, having first cleared the brick joint of mortar. You then set about inserting a very thin membrane. This was where the real skill lay: in making sure it was always properly overlapped. Then, after treating both ends, one had to reinforce the brick course above by the clever use of special slates – all this in a space only a quarter of an inch wide. Afterwards, you went inside the house, located the same course and reversed the procedure, making sure that the existing membrane was fully overlapped. When the job was completed, it was checked and passed by the foreman.

Although I was working in the familiar environment of a building site, I found some of the two lads' habits rather disconcerting. For instance, at home in Dublin the brew-up at ten o'clock was looked forward to with great expectation; I always likened it to the moment when a reluctant swimmer, having plunged in and got over the initial shock, happily sits on the side of the pool for a breather. Also, the ten o'clock tea-break helped many a man to complete his breakfast, judging by the rashers and sausages one would often see protruding from between two cuts of bread. One of the differences on this job was that we didn't brew up on the site. Instead, we all went to a local café – or caff, as they called all restaurants – where the others surprised and annoyed me by drinking coffee and eating nothing. At lunchtime it was the same, except that they would have a bacon sandwich each.

On Fridays, when Mr Flanagan called to the job, we all trooped down to the caff again; the lads gave him a run-down on the job in hand, and he paid us and ordered coffee and sandwiches for four. On the first Friday, I cried off the bacon and asked for an egg sandwich instead.

'Why, Billy?' asked Mr Flanagan. 'Do you not like bacon?'

'Why, yes, of course I do, only on Fridays I don't eat meat,' I said, thinking he would understand, as everyone back in Ireland would.

But Mr Flanagan looked genuinely puzzled. 'I don't understand,' he said.

So my temporary landlord spoke up. 'Billy is RC,' he said, by way of explanation.

'RC? What's that mean?' asked Mr Flanagan, his puzzlement showing clearly on his face.

'It means he's a Roman Catholic, and in their religion they don't eat meat on Fridays.'

The coffees and sandwiches arrived, and while Mr Flanagan paid the girl I tucked into my egg sandwich with eager anticipation. Having finished, I sat back and lit my pipe.

Through the blue haze I saw Mr Flanagan still staring at me. Then he said, 'I know nothing of religion, having been brought up an agnostic, so tell me, Billy: why do you abstain from eating meat on a Friday?'

'Because it was on a Friday that Jesus Christ was crucified,' I said, happy in the knowledge that I was helping an unbeliever to understand the teachings of the Catholic Church.

'Yes,' he said, 'but why do you abstain from eating meat on that day?'

'I do it for penance,' I replied rather smugly.

'Do you now? Well, in my book, Billy, you're nothing but a hypocrite.'

I nearly swallowed my pipe. 'Why do you say that, Mr Flanagan?' I asked.

'I was watching you enjoying your egg sandwich – and I was delighted: but then to tell me you ate it as a form of penance is laughable. I would have thought more of you if you had abstained altogether. As it is, you only changed your diet.'

I looked at him and he laughed out loud. 'As one of your countrymen once said, thank God I'm an agnostic.'

The day I heard that the rule about abstaining from meat on Friday had been abolished, I thought of all the Mr Flanagans and remembered the day I was made to eat humble pie.

One day, as we drove in the van through the heart of London, I commented on the fact that one saw very few bicycles on the roads. The younger Scottish brickie replied, 'Only coloured people ride bikes in London, and if you do see a white person on one, you can bet he's a Paddy.'

I found his light-hearted remark offensive, and didn't hesitate to tell him so. Later, reflecting on it, I sensed that there was a deep-rooted dislike for the Irish among certain Scotsmen – especially Scotsmen living in England – and this showed itself in the form of put-downs. This attitude is very sad, but I believe its basis goes right back in history to that time when England wanted to be the complete master of these so-called British Isles. The Welsh people, with their love of music, singing and their own culture, accepted John Bull for what he was; but the Scots and the Irish rose up and fought the invader. History shows that, after many bloody battles, the Scots accepted defeat; but history also shows that the Irish – who were classed as 'thick' – still do not know the meaning of the word 'defeat'. Am I right, I wonder? Or am I as thick as the land that bred me? Only time and history will tell.

But, even while thinking these thoughts, I could not fault my two Scottish mates. They were very generous with their time and, above all, with their knowledge, which they imparted to me. Also, every Friday they would drop me off at a railway station where I would get the train to Wood Green; then I would get two buses and arrive, late on Friday night, in Mitchem Surrey, where my sister Margaret lived with Doug, her English-born husband, and their young family.

When I went home, it was coming into late November. The two Scottish lads played Santa Claus, buying presents for each of my three children. After being there for six weeks, I was very glad to be going home; but I was really sorry to be saying good-bye to two such great mates and their families, who had accepted me as one of their own. 'Like ships that pass in the night,' I thought, as I reflected on the last six weeks and the bond of friendship that had allowed the three of us to work as mates, sharing our knowledge, our thoughts and a lot of sweet laughter. Now here I was, alone and adrift again.

In the darkness of the night, the boat I was travelling on slowly pulled out from the Liverpool dock and headed out into the Irish Sea. I was going home. Thinking of the two lads and the brief friendship we had shared, I penned these few words.

We met for a brief moment
In life's eternal time,
When you extended the hands of friendship,
And I clutched them both in mine.
For friendship such as ours
Is not measured by the years –
Its foundation lies in its laughter
Cemented by life's bitter tears.

CHAPTER 19

My Time in Trinity

When the boat docked at the North Wall, at around 7.30am, I could not help noticing the quietness and the lack of people moving about on the docks and elsewhere in the city. Finding it difficult to get a taxi, I contrasted this with London, where many people were on the move from six o'clock in the morning. I suppose in those days Dublin was still a provincial town that viewed strangers with a certain amount of innate suspicion. When I finally did succeed in getting a taxi, the driver's first words to me were not 'Where are you going?' but 'Where are you from?'

When I mentioned Crumlin, his face suddenly beamed. 'I have a brother living out there. Are you long there yourself?'

'Yes, all my life,' I replied.

'Then you must be one of the locals?' he asked, with that assured air that meant, 'Before I get you home I'll even find out who your father was.'

Again I found myself noticing the contrast. Only a few miles separate us from mainland Britain, yet in customs, habits and outlook we were poles apart. In London, no one would give a toss where you came from or where you were going; their unfailing good manners, or maybe their complete indifference, would never allow them to inquire into your private life. In Ireland, on the other hand, people love to know what you had for your breakfast, dinner and tea, and then have the nerve to tell you that 'what you have for supper is your own business'. They are a strange people, my people.

I arrived home to a wonderful reception from my wife and young children. After breakfast, having a few extra bob in my pocket, I suggested that we all go into town to see Santa Claus. Of course this was met with shouts of joy and approval.

Standing outside Santa's grotto in Clery's, I spied Santa with a letter in his hand, looking a bit perplexed. Then I spotted a studious-looking young boy gazing up at Santa with a puzzled look, while his well-to-do parents stood proudly nearby. 'Jaysus, I'm in trouble,' muttered Santa through his beard, glancing at me. 'This bloody chiseler wants me to read his letter, and I can't see an effin' thing without me glasses.' Laughing out loud, I suddenly realised that I was really and truly home again in Dublin.

When I reported to Thompson's in Fairview the next morning, I was questioned by one of the bosses, a Mr Goody. He kindly asked me how my young family had reacted to me walking in the door after being away for six long weeks; then, having given me tea, he kindly suggested that I take the rest of the day off. The next day I was to report to a Mr Murphy in Lever Bros; their factory was at that time situated down on the docks, and was known locally as 'Castleforbes soap factory'.

As I pushed my bike in the main gate next morning, the first thing that met my eye was a small altar decorated with lights and flowers. On inquiring, I was told that the altar was on the very spot where Matt Talbot had worked nearly forty years before, when it was Martin's timber yard. Thinking back to the time when, as a sixteen-year-old youth, I had worked in Granby Lane where he had died, and now seeing the very spot where he once actually stood and worked, was somehow disturbing. It was as if an inexplicable circle was slowly being formed around my working life. When I was young, I always believed that man had free will to do whatever and go wherever he liked; but, since entering my thirties and being exposed to the teaching of the Jesuits, I had begun to realise that we human beings have very little say in our own destinies.

In those days, all the papers were full of the very recent assassination of President Kennedy. Here was a man who at that time was the most powerful and arguably the most popular man in the western world; a young man endowed with lots of charm, good looks and a beautiful wife and young family – and, though he was guarded day and night by FBI agents armed with guns, yet this young man whose life held such promise was gunned down in broad daylight in front of thousands of his fellow men. At the time I could not help wondering if those two men, Matt Talbot and President J.F. Kennedy – poles apart in social status, education and time – had shared the same vision. In 1925, when he died on the streets of Dublin, poor Matt Talbot was a nobody, yet almost immediately after his death, he was being venerated and many people prayed to him to intercede to God Almighty on their behalf; whereas President Kennedy, after he died on a Dallas street, was much maligned. Yet each man, in his own way, caused a ripple in the still waters we call life.

I was happy working in Castleforbes factory. I had arrived just as Thompson was building a large extension, and there were two other bricklayers working with me, so the craic and the money were good. Most of the people working in the factory came from around the docklands and were known as 'Eastwallers', as distinct from people of the Liberties, Ringsend or the Five Lamps. Each of these groups was almost tribal in their assertiveness that they, and they alone, were the 'real Dubs'. Also, each group was very protective of its own, viewing strangers like me as complete outsiders, foreigners from outside the pale. These feelings, I found, were still very strong, even in the Swinging Sixties – although I have to say the so-called Swinging Sixties had little effect on thousands of people like me, whose only vices were getting up early every morning and cycling into work to earn money to buy food for their families.

It has to be said, however, that President Kennedy's visit to our country in June that year had given us a great feeling; we were like a nation reawakening after a long sleep. This was seen in the rise of the showbands and the ballad groups like The Dubliners, The Chieftains and The Wolfe Tones; even in America, the Clancy Brothers and Tommy Makem were helping to put Irish ballads on the international stage. And, of course, public-house owners, suddenly seeing gold instead of sawdust, immediately opened their old back rooms – which they renamed 'lounges' – and, with undue haste, imported unknown groups from Kildare and even further afield. It was strange to hear again these old songs, songs I had heard my mother sing as she washed the clothes in a bath balanced on a chair, her scrubbing board immersed in water carried from the village pump. Is it any wonder that these songs evoked, in all of the old and not so old, feelings of nostalgia for our disappearing youth?

Even the Ancient Guild of Incorporated Brick and Stone-layers' Union was not immune to this new ballad scene. At one very stormy meeting, the members were debating the loss of revenue and suggested that a subcommittee be appointed to make use of the hall and its many facilities. Many names were proposed before Kevin Thornberry, John Geraty, Patrick Gahan, James Maguire, Mick McCarthy and I were appointed. Most of us disagreed with one another's views; but, by a stroke of luck, at our first meeting Mick McCarthy proposed Kevin Thornberry as chairman. Kevin was about the best chairman I had ever had the pleasure of working with. Being older than us hotheads, he kept us in check, but he allowed us to follow up on our often over-the-top suggestions. Thanks to Kevin, after a period of time we became a close-knit group. It was during this time that Mick McCarthy and I became firm friends, especially when he began to organise some concerts with that great Kerry storyteller Eamonn Kelly – or the *Scealaíocht*, as he was referred to in the Kingdom.

Meanwhile, I was kept busy by my new employer. It soon emerged that Castleforbes was not the only job he was engaged in. Over a period of months I found myself working in the Ulster Banks in O'Connell Street and in Blackrock, in Trinity College, and in Maguire and Patterson, the famous Irish match company. Working in all these various places gave me a broader view of the commercial and academic life of the city than I would have gained if I had been confined to a regular building site. For instance, working in the match factory was fascinating to me – just seeing those huge tree-trunks coming in through the back doors of the timber yard and then, after a short time, seeing the same timber, literally reduced to matchwood, going out the main front doors in thousands of small boxes.

Unfortunately, my memories of working in Trinity College are of a less academic nature than I would have wished. They dwell on more mundane things – like the time one of the old retainers of the firm (we called him Mouth Almighty, because you could hear him long before you saw him) accidentally broke a window in one of the College buildings while carrying a ladder up some stairs. Having admitted to breaking the window, he begged me to get on the phone and tell Mr Thompson what had happened. I, being the noble type, immediately said no; I suggested he phone the boss himself.

Mouth Almighty was not a phone man. This met with the response I expected: 'Ring the boss? On the phone? Are yeh mad or somethin'? Sure, I never used one of them bloody things in me life.'

'Please yourself; but, as foreman, I'll have to tell Mr Thompson when he arrives on the job after lunch that the window is broken. He'll ask how that happened, and I'll have to tell him it was you that broke it.'

A crafty gleam slowly appeared in Mouth's eye, and he had the nerve to wink it at me. 'Couldn't yeh just say some chiseler must have thrown a stone at it?'

'No, I couldn't,' I said, drawing myself up to my five foot whatever and trying to be serious in front of the two draughtsmen working in the office. 'You have a nerve, asking me to lie for you.'

'Aye, sure, it wouldn't be the first time yeh lied, yeh little cur,' Mouth Almighty said with real terror in his voice.

'What do you mean by that?' I cried in mock horror. The poor devil was nearly in a state of shock over breaking the window; what he didn't know was that it had already been listed as cracked and was due to be replaced anyway.

'I didn't mean what I said,' he muttered, walking around and around in circles.

'No, I'm afraid I can't accept that,' I said. 'You said it wasn't the first time I lied; now explain yourself.'

Mouth looked at me, then at the ground, and muttered, 'Well, they were talking the other day about you and all the jobs you're supposed to be a expert on – damp-coursing, stonework, boiler work, laying out jobs of all kinds... You can cod the others, but I'm tellin' yeh the human brain can only hold so much, and you're well over the limit, yeh little effer.'

I laughed at his words, but I still decided to go ahead with getting him to ring the builder. So, going into the other office, I rang up the head office and explained the set-up to one of the lads; he, knowing Mouth Almighty well, immediately said he would pretend to be Mr Thompson. Then I approached Mouth. 'You're in deep trouble,' I said, trying to look stern.

'How?' he asked, nearly shitting himself.

'I've got Mr Thompson on the phone, so you'd better

explain to him about breaking that window,' I said, handing him the phone.

'What end do I talk into?' asked the poor devil, handling the phone like a terrified rookie soldier would handle a live hand grenade.

'That end there,' I said. 'Just hold it up to your mouth and talk into it. The boss is at the other end, waiting to talk to you.'

With trembling hands Mouth Almighty took the phone. 'Hello, Mr Thompson,' he bellowed into it. 'I've somethin' to tell you. I – I broke one – one of the windows in the College, sir.'

The lad posing as Mr Thompson must have asked him what size the window was, because Mouth suddenly dropped the phone and, indicating with his hands, stammered, 'Only – only a little bastard, that size, sir.' I handed him back the phone; he held it to his ear in complete silence, nodding now and then, a very serious look on his face. After about three minutes of listening, he handed the phone back to me. 'Well, I told him.'

Trying to keep a straight face, I asked, 'Now are you glad that you told Mr Thompson about the window?'

'No, I'm not,' Mouth muttered under his breath, fixing his greasy cap at an acute angle on his head.

'But it's all over now,' I said. 'It's water under the bridge.'

'Water under the bridge, me arse,' said he, making for the door. 'Isn't he after atin' the shite out of me for the last half-hour – and there was nothin' watery about that!' Then, banging the door behind him, he was gone; and I was left with a memory – twisted, some might say, but joyful nevertheless – that re-runs itself in my mind whenever I happen to pass Trinity College.

Mouth Almighty always viewed me with suspicion, and I, knowing this, fed him with great big lies. Having told the lie, I would always say to him, 'Ah, that's as true as I'm riding this bicycle' – even though I'd be standing beside him without a bicycle in sight. One time I said to him, 'I'm going to tell you something in complete confidence, and I don't want you to breathe a word to anyone else. I'm really a tailor – but the price of needles has gone up so much in the last year, I thought it would be cheaper to be a bricklayer.' The very next day, an old plasterer said to me, 'Billy, were you really a tailor?' As my grandfather used to say, 'A good lie is never wasted – not when there's always some gobshite out there willing to believe it.'

As I mentioned, I also worked in two Ulster Banks for the same firm. Working in the Blackrock branch was enjoyable and rewarding, in terms of both money and work. There was brick and cut stone to be laid outside, and, because we could only work inside when they closed the bank at three, we were able to chalk up some worthwhile overtime. The job inside the bank consisted of laying and bedding Italian processed tiles on the floor. These highly polished tiles were a bastard size, something like thirteen and a half inches square, and great care had to be exercised in the cutting of them. Also, the internal walls were finished with beauty board and sprang from the same tile, cut to act as skirting, so that we had to become very proficient in the art of tile-cutting.

The Ulster Bank in O'Connell Street was a different kettle of fish. We never saw the inside of the bank. They brought a lad over from London for a few days to show us how to wash and clean down the old stonework that fronts the bank, using acid and cold water in the proper proportions. In those winter days, we worked outside on scaffolding in appalling conditions, with no protective clothing provided – like the pilots in the First World War, who were not allowed to wear parachutes in case they might jump out of their planes at the first sight of the enemy. As a result, between supervising and working with the lads at the stone-cleaning, I caught a cold that soon developed into pneumonia.

CHAPTER 20

A County Cow Brickie

During the six long weeks that I was ill, not one member of the firm that employed me came through my hall door to inquire as to how I was. And the sin was, I accepted this as part of the normal social structure that existed at that time.

My only income during those terrible six weeks was the less-than-adequate sick benefit, plus a very small weekly cheque from the Union; these, when combined, could benefit nobody but the undertakers. I was seriously ill and needed extra little comforts, like a doctor and medicines. But my wife was told that the fact that I was paying for welfare stamps (the cost of which had always been taken from my earnings before I received my pay packet, from the time I was sixteen) did not in itself entitle me to a free doctor or to any medicines whatsoever. To qualify for such luxuries, it appears, I should never have gone out to work at all. There was also the little matter of buying food for my wife and growing family. Yet, even in my sickness, or maybe because of it, I somehow had not the heart to call my family together and tell them to stop eating.

I'm sure the public at large, especially the politicians, get sick and tired hearing about the gripes of the working man. But I had worked all my life and never cost the State one penny – only contributed to it by my own skills – only to be told that, if I had never bothered to work in the first place, I could have had a free doctor and all the medication required to make me well again, so that I would be able to walk down to the Social Welfare office under my own steam to collect the weekly cheque that would allow me to continue doing nothing. This is called social justice. 'We must look after the poor and the needy,' the Church and State proclaim; but what about the much-reviled working man? Could nobody in the so-called Social Services at that time arrange for a man who had paid for twenty years' worth of welfare stamps to be given his full wages and free medical care while he was out of the workplace because of a genuine sickness? Would that have taxed their feeble brains, or upset their half-yearly figures?

After five long weeks between the bed and the sofa I ventured out – only to find that my poor legs, which had over the years supported me so well on bicycle and scaffolding, were unable to carry my newly thin body for even a few yards. After the initial shock – and it was a terrible shock to find, at the age of thirty-six, that I was now a feeble person – I decided that, whatever the consequences, it was time I got up off my skinny little arse and rejoined the world.

With the help of my doctor and Maeve, I began to gently ease into a daily routine of exercise that helped me to find the use of my legs again – only to discover that somewhere along the way I had lost my bloody hearing. Talk about being bewitched, bothered and bewildered.

One day, in the course of trying to walk normally, I arrived outside the brickies' hall in Cuffe Street gasping for breath, and collided with Frank O'Connor, the General Secretary of the union.

'Begob, Billy,' said he, 'you're a ghost.'

I, deeply depressed, replied, 'Surely I'm not that bad-looking, Frank?'

'No, I didn't mean it like that,' he said, laughing. 'No, what I meant was that I was just thinking of you. A good friend of mine, a Mr Bolton from the Dublin County Council, was on the phone only an hour or two ago looking for a bricklayer;

and, knowing you were recovering from your illness, I thought it might suit you. I can give you a letter of introduction if you like.'

I, seeing myself on the road back to normality, cried out in my mind, 'Yes, yes please, oh, yes please!'

Later that same day, clutching the precious letter, I arrived at the depot in the townland of Robinhood, near the village of Clondalkin. I met and spoke to Mr Pat Bolton; after asking me the usual questions about my work experience, he said, 'Could you start work next Monday morning at eight-thirty?' I nodded my head vigorously in the definite direction of a yes.

I was then left with the task – and it was not a small one – of telling Maeve, my doctor, and Thompson's. They all reacted as I expected them to: with a large 'No way!' It took a lot of persuasion on my part to convince them all that this was what I felt I had to do. I just had to get back to work and normality.

Arriving in the Council yard on Monday morning, I was introduced to a Jim Dorneen, who was to be my mate. He very soon became much, much more than that: he became one of my closest friends. Jim put me right on who to watch in the County Cow, as we called it – in that year of '64, the Dublin County Council area was so rural and had so few houses that the bin-cars collected the refuse twice weekly from the same houses, and horses and carts were still used on the roads.

My first job for the Council was building a pair of block piers to carry a large gate at the entrance to the new dump, way out in Cabinteely. After Jim had supervised the loading of the blocks, mortar, cement, shovels and tools, one of the drivers brought us out to the site. Arriving there, I soon realised that, after sitting in the van for so long, my legs refused point blank to perform for the Council. It was as if they were acting up because they hadn't been notified that I had gone back to work before my body was ready.

So all I could do was to take this stranger, Jim Dorneen, into my confidence. His reaction was typical of the man I came to love and trust. Mixing out the muck, he built the two piers block upon block, only asking me to plumb them and point up the joints. In between, he lit a fire and made the finest mug of tea that I had enjoyed in many a day. After only a few days of Jim's minding, I felt strong enough to tackle other jobs.

There was, of course, a down-side to all of this, and that was the take-home pay. While working as a foreman in Thompson's, what with a bit of overtime and travelling time, I had taken home about twenty pounds a week; the first week's wages I got from the County Council, after working a back week, was about eleven pounds.

I talked this over with Mr Bolton, who advised me not to do anything hasty; the next day he gave me the address of a relation of his who wanted some walls built. Over a period of time, I must have built nearly every garden wall in the Wainsfort and Templeogue area. This was called nixering, and was frowned on by the Union; but it was a perfect and honest way to bring up your money to a living wage. It was also very hard work.

After I had been working for the County Council for about three months, they issued me a pair of Wellington boots, overalls and a raincoat. I was delighted; it was the first time I had ever got anything in the way of clothing from an employer. The raincoat was a black, rubbery kind without pockets, which I thought rather appropriate: due to the small wage they gave you, you would have no money to put in the pockets anyway!

I was still very active on the Union subcommittee, and was shocked when I heard that our own chairman, Kevin Thornberry, who had just been promoted to Inspector of Dangerous Buildings, had suffered a blood clot in the head. I went to see him in hospital, and he seemed to be coming along OK. When I arrived at the hall one evening for a meeting, I was delighted to be told that Kevin was inside. As I approached him, I noticed that he looked well: his curly copper hair shone in the semi-darkness of the large room, and he seemed happy to be among his friends again.

'Hello, Kevin,' I said as I reached for his hand. 'How are you?'

'Great,' he said, looking hard at me. 'Where are you at it now?' I knew there and then that he didn't know me.

'I'm in the County Cow,' I stuttered.

This seemed to trigger something in his brain. 'Do you ever see Billy French?' he asked.

I went along with him. 'Yes, I see him most days.'

Kevin's eyes lit up, and that lovely roguish smile that I knew so well appeared on his face. 'When you see him again, tell him I was asking for him.' Then he seemed to go into himself again. 'Christ,' he muttered, more to himself than to me, 'we used to have laughs – the things we did...' He paused, as if thinking about the times we had shared when we were young and game for almost anything. Soon afterwards, when I was attending his funeral, I thought long and deeply about Kevin's remarks.

When you are facing your own demise, does the mind, instead of slowly winding down, go back to happier times, when you were young and life was full of expectation? And is it in that frame of mind that you embrace your new life beyond the grave? As the Kerryman would say, I'd love to know, but I'm not dying to find out – not just yet.

After I had been in the job for about six months, Mr Bolton asked me if I would be prepared to drive a van myself out to the various jobs that had to be attended to. I immediately agreed. Because of the nature of the work, we could cover a greater area in the same day if I was driving our own van. It also gave Jim and me greater freedom. He could load the van with whatever we wanted – blocks, bricks, sand and cement – the evening before, so that, after reporting in the next morning, we could head out to Lucan, Bohernabreena or Bray without any hassle.

This was a very happy period of my working life, and I look back on it with great fondness. In my mind I can see, quite clearly, the two of us sitting on large stones covered with age in an old graveyard in Cabinteely, Jim with his cigarette and me with my pipe, the two of us looking at the wall we had just completed – using the original old stones – and comparing it to the old wall we had tied it in to.

Jim was a big Wexford man who had started out as a gardener, and his knowledge of nature and bird life never ceased to amaze me. He was also full of dry sayings. I remember once we were building an extension to the Lucan town toilets; having completed the brickwork outside, we moved inside, where the partition walls were removed so that the plumber could work on the three toilet pans. Jim was missing one day, and when he reappeared I said to him, 'Where have you been?' – even though I knew only too well that he had nipped into the local bookie's to back a horse.

Jim looked at me, then at the three toilet pans standing naked without the protection of their partition walls. 'I can't say I was in the toilet, now can I?' said he with a silly grin on his face.

Shortly after we completed the job, I was informed by Dublin County Council that my application for the job of Assistant Foreman of Works had been successful.

CHAPTER 21

Wearing the Good Suit

So it was that, on a bright Monday morning in September 1966, I – for the first time in my working career – arrived on a job without my tools or overalls, to take up my duties as Assistant Foreman of Works.

The list of duties was off-putting, to say the least. First off, I found myself in charge of forty-nine men – bin-men, tradesmen, store-men, watchmen and drivers. My first duty was to allocate work; then I had to get the men out of the yard every morning as soon as possible, check work times, sign their sheets and regulate holidays. I was also responsible for the maintenance of all dumps, bin-cars, lorries and vans. I had to hire the machines and see that Bohernabreena, Esker, Cruigh and Templeogue burial-grounds, plus eight old graveyards, were maintained in a proper manner, which included the laying of new paths and the cutting of grass twice a year. My wages for carrying out these duties, I was informed by letter, amounted to £14.11s.2d per week, fully inclusive.

The County Council in those days extended from Shankill to Balbriggan, and was divided into three main sections. John Morley was doing similar work to me in the vast area from Balbriggan to Clonee; I was in charge of the area from the Salmon Leap, on the borders of Kildare, out to Rathfarnham; and John Prior carried out a similar service from Rathfarnham to Bray. Each of these three areas was expanding at a frightening rate, with, as I saw it, not a thought for conservation of any kind. Trees and natural resources that had been home to all kinds of wildlife for hundreds of years were disappearing before our eyes under the relentless wheels of ever bigger machines, and the sadness was that no one said stop. We – all of us – are to blame.

Among the tradesmen I was responsible for were a carpenter and a painter, both of whom had been established in their jobs long before I came along. What I needed was a good reliable bricklayer to carry out the work I had been doing when on my tools.

In one of those unexplainable twists that happen in life, one day I took a wrong turn on my way home, only to see the bold Jim Garland walking along the Killeen Road. When I stopped him, I saw right away that he was a very troubled man.

'What's wrong with you?' I said. 'You look as if you've lost a pound and found a penny.'

'It's worse than that,' he said. 'They're reorganising the whole mill, and, as I see it, most of the lads like myself will be out of a job soon.'

'Is that all?' I said, laughing. 'I thought you were going to tell me something serious.'

He looked hard at me, as if wondering whether I had been drinking. 'It's not funny, Billsyer,' he muttered. 'Where am I going to get a job at my age? I just couldn't keep up with them young brickies on piece-work. Them little bastards would run rings round me.'

I laughed out loud as I pictured Jim trying to acclimatise himself to the raw building conditions, especially after working in the intense heat of the boilers for all those years. 'Well, Jim,' I said, 'let's face it: you're finished, washed up – that is, of course, unless you want to work under me in the County Council.'

As my words sank in, I could actually see the strain lift from his face. 'You're not kiddin', Billsyer, are yeh?'

'No, old friend, I'm not kiddin', as you say. I'm remembering the time when I was desperate for work and you were responsible for me getting six good years in the mill.'

Jim's eyes misted over as he put his hand on my shoulder, and I, embarrassed, said rather gruffly, 'Report to me at Robin Hood Depot next Monday morning at half past eight.'

As I drove off, I shouted, 'Don't be late – and don't forget to call me "sir"!'

Looking in the rear-view mirror, all I could see was Jim doubled up laughing, and again I was reminded of those strange circles that seem to direct and govern our lives.

One advantage of having worked as a brickie in the yard was that I heard the gripes of the men as they sat around eating their sandwiches and drinking scalding tea from a black can. It's impossible, in any workplace where men are gathered, to avoid the long-held grievances, imaginary or otherwise, that invade the best of workforces, and these men working out of Robin Hood Depot in all weathers were no different.

One of the most consistent complaints, which reared its head time and time again, was the Dublin County Council's policy of paying the men's weekly wages through the post. The post often arrived at their homes too late on Fridays for them to cash their cheques at the bank, so a lot of these men had to go to their local shops on Saturday morning to get their cheques changed. These men, the old residents (or 'non-runners-in', as they classed themselves) of Oldcourt, Firhouse, Tallaght and the hills of Bohernabreena, were fiercely defensive of their own privacy; and all, without exception, told stories of shopkeepers who, as they changed the cheques, would remark out loud about the amount of money on the cheque. If this sum was up or down, because of overtime or a rise in their weekly pay, this too would be mentioned by some busybody shopkeeper. So, when I became foreman, I immediately set about putting this major gripe to rights. All it entailed was approaching the Wages Officer, explaining the problem, and suggesting that I go in every Thursday after lunch and pick up all the cheques, so that the men could collect them at the Depot before they went home. He, being a very reasonable man, immediately agreed to my suggestion, and that simple system worked quite well for the remainder of my time in the Depot.

One of the major tasks that confronted me as Foreman of Works was learning the routes of all bin-cars in my jurisdiction, and then trying to juggle all the routes periodically to allow for new houses in rapidly expanding places like Tallaght, Lucan and Clondalkin. This, as expected, caused a lot of aggravation among older bin-men who had been lifting the same bins in that same area long before I came into the yard. How did I know this? They constantly told me so!

Being a Foreman of Works in a local authority was, I soon found out, vastly different from being a foreman on a building site. In my time as a builder, I had worked alongside men who openly admitted to having done time in jail for robbery and other violent crimes; but, once they did the job that they were being paid for, nobody would dream of looking down his nose at them. The attitude seemed to be 'There but for the grace of God go I.' But when I first went into Dublin County Council, local TDs and parish priests were still writing letters to secure employment for certain people who would not get or hold jobs on their own merits. This was brought home to me very forcefully shortly after I took up my new appointment.

The situation concerned a bin-man. This particular man always went absent every Friday, and I would then have to direct one of the spare men to take his place. All the spare men, with few exceptions, were former bin-men who now worked in the burial-grounds or at any other such work that might arise. As a bin-car can only go as fast as the slowest man, the bin crew resented having to take an older man on board. So one Thursday evening I informed this individual that if he was absent the next day, he had better not come in on Monday morning without a note from his doctor. As I expected, he did not report for work on Friday. The following Monday morning, as he was getting into the bin-car, I asked him where he had been on Friday.

'That's my business,' he said, turning his back on me.

'No,' I said, 'it's my business. Have you a medical cert?'

'No.'

'In that case, you're fired.' I turned to one of the spare men. 'You're working on that car from now on.' Having said my piece, I went back into the office.

The next morning, who should arrive in the yard as the bin-men were leaving but our work-shy friend. 'I was told to give you this before I started back to work,' he said, handing me a brown envelope. Opening it, I was amazed to read that I was to reinstate this individual immediately, on pain of death, etcetera, etcetera... It was signed by a well-known local politician. I was very conscious of the rest of the men looking on, and I knew this demanded some kind of a gesture on my part.

'Will you be seeing this gentleman again?' I inquired.

'Yes, I've to tell him what happened.'

'Good. You won't have much to tell him.' I held the letter out at arm's length, tore it into little strips and threw it up in the air. Then I turned to the painter, who was grinning from ear to ear, and gave him his instructions for the day.

The next Monday morning, I brought in all the lads' sheets to be co-signed by the engineer. As he scrutinised them, he said, 'I had a very irritated gentleman on the phone the other day, saying you sacked one of his party workers and demanding to know what I was going to do about it.'

'And what did you tell him?' I asked, rather apprehensively.

Mr Byrne flashed me one of his rare smiles and continued to sign the sheets. 'I just told our illustrious caller that, now that the lad no longer worked for the Dublin County Council, he would have more time to work for the party.' Strange – we never heard another word about it.

Another time I caught the crew of a bin-car loading stuff other than domestic refuse and had to hand them a three-day suspension. But it was not all doom and gloom. There were some very funny moments that I still remember – like the time Tom the bin-man fell off the back of his bin-car.

It happened like this. After a number of years of having side-loading cars which had to be unloaded five or six times a day, we were eventually given six modern back-loaders, which, due to their size, could collect and carry much more refuse, so that the lads only had to drive to the dump twice a day. But one day Tom ended up being brought to hospital in an ambulance. After undergoing tests, he was released; but I'm sure he fell on his head, for when he came into the office next morning to make a claim, I got the distinct feeling he thought I had the compensation locked in my desk.

'Can I make a claim?' he asked.

'Certainly, as long as your claim is valid.'

'Course it is... what you said. Didn't I fall off the bloody bin-car?' he said, rubbing his back and anywhere else his hand could reach. 'Sure, amn't I'm bloody sore all over?'

Handing him a large form, I told him to take it home with him, fill it in and bring it back to me the following morning. Now Tom, like a lot of workmen of that period, was not too happy in the company of pencils or pens; so, thrusting the form back at me, he winked and whispered, 'Fill it out yourself, Billy – I'll forgive you any mistakes that you make.'

But I was adamant. 'No,' I said. 'When the case goes to court, the first thing they'll do is test your handwriting against the writing on this form.'

He looked at me, then muttered sarcastically, 'I suppose you'll be tellin' me next that they'll test the skid-marks on the road to see if they match the skid-marks on me arse.' Then, grabbing the form from my hand, he stormed out, slamming the office door behind him.

Next morning, one of the drivers put his head around the door. He, like Tom, lived in the hills of Bohernabreena. 'Hey, Billy,' he whispered, 'you're going to get a bestseller handed to you this morning.'

'What do you mean?' I asked, rather puzzled.

'Well, I was out looking at a few sheep of mine that were about to drop their lambs – about two in the morning, it was – and I glanced across at Tom's house. The light was still burning in his window – and that wasn't all: there appeared to be ink-stains all over the place.'

Shortly afterwards, Tom handed me the completed form. After reading it, I duly brought it into the head office in Parnell Square and gave it to one of the girls. She read it and burst out laughing. It was then passed around from person to person, and each time it met with the same response.

This is, roughly, Tom's account of falling off the bin-car.

'Sir. We had finished for the day and we were heading back to the dump. I was standing on the step at the back of the bin-car when it came to the humpy bridge just outside Newcastle. The car was travelling fairly fast and I must have been holding on rather loosely for I was suddenly put up in the air. When I came down the bin-car was gone.'

Someone suggested that, in view of the distance he had fallen, Tom should apply for extra travelling time instead of for compensation. But I'm glad to report that he lived well into his eighties, none the worse for his infamous fall.

During my working life, I was lucky to meet certain people who enriched my life – people who did not fit into any known category, and who therefore would be regarded as characters.

But I always believed that those people were not just characters, but true artists; and, like all artists, they each developed their own style.

I recall one such character who worked in the County Council depot. His name was Bill, and he was always very definite in his utterings, whether they were true or not – and usually they were not; but he had this special knack of convincing people, especially those in authority, that what he said was gospel.

One day an engineer called me and told me to have Bill report to him when he came into the yard, which I duly did. It transpired that the engineer had driven past Bill's house at twelve-thirty that afternoon and had spotted Bill's bicycle parked outside. 'And I drove by your house again at two o'clock, only to find your bicycle still parked outside.' The engineer added sarcastically, 'By God, man, it must be some dinner your wife gives you, if it takes you an hour and a half to eat it!'

Without even a moment's hesitation, Bill answered, 'Oh, no, sir; you see, the dinner she gives me is harmless, but she always goes to town on the dessert.'

The engineer looked at him sharply; then, slowly turning his back on old Bill, he whispered to me, 'Get him out of here.'

Another time we were discussing World War I, and I mentioned that my uncle Jack had lost his life in that so-called Great War. Then Bill butted in and said that his oldest brother Ben was the very first soldier, from either side, to be killed in France in 1914.

'How can you be sure?' inquired one of the drivers. 'Was your family notified of that fact officially?'

Bill's reply was, as usual, quite definite, without even the slightest hint of ambiguity. 'No, not officially,' he said, lighting his bent-shank pipe. 'But we got it from the horse's mouth, so to speak.'

'How?' I asked.

'Well, sure, didn't the brother himself tell us when he came home on leave?' said Bill – and, even though his mouth was full of tobacco smoke, his voice carried such conviction that nobody had the heart to argue with him.

In those far-off days, when the Health Board reported the body of a dead animal such as a dog or a cat lying on some roadway, it was Bill's job to collect and bury the dead animal. For this he was paid the very large sum of five shillings. One morning we got word that a dead donkey was lying on the dual carriageway out near Bray, so I despatched the flat lorry, with lifting gear and two men, including Bill, with orders to bury the animal at least twenty feet deep in a nearby dump.

Later the Health Inspector was in my office, discussing the incident. Bill, spotting him, knocked on the door and, in his best parliamentary voice, inquired of the Health Inspector whether, due to the size of the animal in question, it would be possible for him to be given more than the usual fee of five shillings.

But the Health Inspector was adamant: five shillings was the standard fee. As he was writing the cheque, he asked, 'As a matter of interest, Bill, where do you bury the dead animals?'

Again without a moment's hesitation, Bill gave one of his stock answers: 'Approximately two metres from the scene of death, sir.'

His answer was immediately accepted by the Inspector, who handed over the cheque, while I had visions of poor old Bill, with his pick and shovel, trying to bury that dead jackass in the centre of a very busy dual carriageway.

One Christmas Eve, one of the men was found dead in his cottage. What with the Christmas holidays, and trying to trace his relations – who turned out to be non-existent – and then having to make the arrangements ourselves, it was about a week before we finally buried the poor man. As we walked out of the graveyard after the burial, which had been attended only by his fellow workers, I spotted old Bill lighting his pipe. 'Well, we buried him like a king,' he said.

'How?' I asked.

'Sure, wasn't he lying in state for six days?'

The same Bill, like most of these characters, lived to a great old age, and died peacefully in his sleep in his own bed. As he lived next to the local graveyard, you could say without fear of contradiction that we buried him approximately two metres from the scene of death.

During the five and a half years I held the title of Assistant Foreman of Works, I completed a two-year course in Supervision and Foremanship in the College of Industrial Relations, between 1967 and 1969. I received two certificates. The College was good enough to notify the engineering staff of the Dublin County Council, and they brought me in to congratulate me. Of course I, being who I was, then informed them that, of all the students to qualify, I was the only one who had had to pay for the full course out of my own pocket!

Because of their isolation, a lot of the older people at that time spoke a curious mixture of English and Irish. This was because, in garrison towns like Kilkenny and Cork, the people had had to learn English quickly so that they could trade with the English soldiers; but in remote places like Bohernabreena, Oldcourt and Firhouse, even though they were on the doorstep of Dublin town, the people carried on their old customs and ways of speaking into the twentieth century. The result was that, when the older people spoke to you, their words were almost directly translated from the Gaeilge.

I remember when one bin-man's father died; as he and his brother were about six foot three, I asked, 'Was your father a big man?' Now, a Dublin man, if asked the same question, would have answered, 'Yeh.' But not Michael; even in his sorrow, he painted a picture in words for me. In his old-fashioned, cultured and sensitive voice, he answered, 'It was said of him, Billy boy, that when he was a young *buachaill* in his prime, it would have been quicker to walk round him than over him. It was also said that his kindness and his *cabhair* [help] were equal to his size.'

I also remember with great fondness two brothers who lived together, drank together and had to work together – no matter what that upstart of a bricklayer turned foreman said. I would send them out to put up some wire fencing; they would work right through the ten o'clock tea break and lunchtime, and then, at about three o'clock, they'd just down tools and say, 'We've done enough for you.' And they meant it.

They lived in an isolated cottage, with about eight dogs of various sizes and pedigrees. One morning when they woke, they found they had been burgled during the night. Arriving in late the next morning, they explained that they had been down to the local police station to report the robbery; but, as the elder brother said, 'Fat lot of good it done us. Bloody policemen – all they believe in is polishing their chairs with their arses.'

I met the local sergeant the next day, and he quickly filled me in on what had happened. It appears that the Chief Superintendent had been visiting the station when the two odd brothers had burst in, shouting that their little cottage had been robbed – a lot of valuables stolen – and it must have been someone they knew, for the eight dogs never barked – and if the police would get off their fat arses immediately, they could catch the robbers!

The Chief Super was livid. 'Then,' said the sergeant, 'I had a brainwave. I reached for the day-book and asked them to produce a current licence for each dog they had. Well, you never saw their heels for dust,' said he, laughing. 'Later that day we found their few valuables scattered around their place. Some small kiddies had done the break-in, after throwing some sweets to the dogs.'

Another time, when the two brothers were working in the local dump, I didn't have a driver available and decided to collect them myself in my new shining Council van. The elder brother, sitting beside me, began to sniff the air.

'What's that smell, Billy?' said he, wrinkling his nose.

'Fresh air,' said I, opening the window.

'You know, that kind of air could kill yeh,' replied the other brother from the back of my spotless blue van.

Being in charge of approximately fifty men for over five years was an experience that I remember with mixed feelings – most of them, I have to admit, happy and enjoyable. These men, by and large, were the salt of the earth. I suppose this was because they literally sprang from the soil.

But suddenly it was 1971, and the job and the world were changing more rapidly than ever before, or so it seemed. For a start, I was forty-three years of age, and I felt my keenness had somehow blunted over the last five and a half years. This was due to several factors. The Sanitary Service Department was expanding at too fast a rate, with more new houses demanding refuse collection every week. Also, many of the old squad of men that I had originally had working under me had retired or died; and the younger ones coming in, it has to be said, hadn't the dedication, the stamina or the experience of the older men, nor the deep interest in what they were doing. I sometimes felt I was having to give more of myself to achieve the required results. Also, management had changed. When I started working in the County Council, the management had consisted of men dedicated to helping you get the best from the workforce; but now there was an influx of so-called whizzkids whose only aim appeared to be, not just to aim for self-made targets, but to then try and surpass these same targets, without regard for or consultation with the people concerned. All these factors led me to believe that it was time for me to move on.

My reasoning was logical. Considering all the responsibilities I had, my weekly wage was a mere pittance in comparison to what good bricklayers were earning in the outside world. Also, my good wife had given birth to our last lovely girl, who was named Maeve after her mother; I felt I owed it to her and to my four children to bring in a decent wage.

As all these thoughts were fermenting within me, there appeared in the national newspapers an advertisement stating that the Dublin County Council was offering six new posts to qualified persons in their Building Control section. The six posts included two General Inspectors, two Inspectors of Plumbing and two Inspectors of Bricklaying. They would be full-time, permanent and pensionable, and I immediately felt that – even though there would be a huge amount of interest among bricklayers – one of those unknown circles that seemed to govern my working life was somehow calling out to be completed. With that in mind, I applied for one of the posts of Inspector of Bricklaying.

CHAPTER 22

Inspector of Bricklaying

I was eventually called for an interview, which was very formal and most detailed, with a lot of searching questions. The panel consisted of three men, one of whom I knew to be a first-class engineer. At the conclusion of the interview, I was asked to draw a house, detailing its construction.

I showed them how, in building a detached house, one should take a level from the crown of the road and transfer those markings to the foundations of the house; your damp-proof course should be laid six inches above that level. I went on to free-draw the main structure, showing the thickness of the outer and inner walls, the placing of the window and door openings, and the spacing of the joists to carry the floors. After drawing the sewage system, I concentrated on the formation of the fireplace, showing how one gathers the various flues into a single stack.

All the time I was drawing, I was being asked questions by the panel. I'll always remember the very last question: 'Tell me, Mr French, what do you call those walls that separate the flue-liners?'

I looked at all three of them, and they stared back at me in a silence that could be heard above the roar of the traffic outside. Then I said light-heartedly, 'I must have been out in the toilet the day they were learning that in the Tech.'

This made two of the men smile, while the other man

repeated the question. At that moment, I remember being amazed at how the brain works: I heard myself repeating, parrot-like, the words dear old Mr Eddie Byrne had taught us in Bolton Street Technical School, all those years ago: 'The walls that separate the flue-liners are called mid-feathers.'

As I was leaving the room, I overheard one of the panel say, 'At least on paper he can build a house,' while I offered a silent prayer of thanks for all the Eddie Byrnes of this life who had taught and shared their knowledge with me.

A few weeks later I received a letter telling me to report to a specialist doctor, appointed by local government, for a medical examination. After going over me from head to toe, the doctor asked me whether my parents were still alive. I answered that my mother was, but that my father was dead. He then asked me – rather abruptly, I thought – how he had died, and added that I was not to tell him lies. I objected to his tone and told him in no uncertain manner that, even if he was in the habit of telling lies, I was not, and that my father had fallen off a scaffolding while working for the Dublin Corporation. He had the grace to apologise. Then, discovering a small varicose vein in my leg, he arranged for me to get it treated, for which I am still grateful to him.

Then, one day in early April, this small but all-important letter arrived for me.

> *A Chara,*
>
> *With reference to previous correspondence, I wish to inform you that the Assistant County Manager by order No. M/81/1971 dated 28/4/1971 has appointed you to the wholetime, permanent and pensionable office of Inspector of Bricklaying with effect from the 10/5/1971, subject to the terms and conditions published. On arrival for duty on Monday, 10th of May, 1971 please report to Mr*

Kevin O'Donnell, Deputy County Engineer, No. 4 Parnell Square.

Of the six inspectors reporting for duty on that day, Danny Gallagher, the other Inspector of Bricklaying, was appointed to the Roads section; John Morley, a General Inspector, was in charge of the north-city Beeches; and the rest of us – Pat Billings, Pat Lynch, Michael Fleming and I – were detailed to report to Building Control, which was then situated in an old building on Dame Street, where the Central Bank stands today.

I initially found it very strange, after five and a half long years of getting other people to carry out my bidding, to be suddenly responsible for no one but myself. It also took me some time to learn the byelaws that related to my job in Building Control; but once I had studied them, and with the kind and generous help of the existing staff, I soon settled in.

After a time we were all shifted out of Dame Street to a new office complex and shopping centre called the Mall, on Lower Abbey Street. On the first morning I arrived at our new offices, I got out of my car and, looking around, realised that I was standing in the old yard of Brook Thomas's – which, in my time as a bricklayer, had been one of the biggest and most comprehensive builder's suppliers in the city of Dublin.

As my memories started to unravel, I set about taking out and filling my pipe – only to be told, by a priggish young man in a posh uniform, that I wasn't allowed to smoke. I looked at him and placed the pipe between my teeth; I continued to stare as he gazed at the blue smoke emerging from the bowl of my old bent-shank pipe. Then I said, 'Son, when I was a young apprentice bricklayer, on many an occasion I pushed a Granby hand-cart into this very yard for to collect a bag of cement, or maybe a few earthenware sewerage pipes and fittings. And this morning I'm coming in here for the first time as an Inspector of Bricklaying, and in my own motor car, too – so be very, very gentle with me, son.'

He looked at me as if to say, 'What's Building Control coming to, when they appoint a shagging oul' fella like that to look after the Council's interests?' And I, knowing what he was thinking, puffed all the more on the stem of my pipe.

For I was thinking of all those great old bricklayers I had met in the course of my journey here, who, by their knowledge, experience and shrewdness – or 'canatness', as the old word is – had made me what I was. Images of my father teaching Johnny, Brendan and me the different bonds, with a pile of old bricks in the back yard, came back very clearly to me. Then other images emerged – of his father, old Ha'-pa'-nine, in that run-down part of old Dublin called the Liberties, hanging out a wet cloth through the window of his tenement room of a winter's night and feeling it the next morning, as nearly all the bricklayers of his generation did; for if the cloth was hard, then it was too frosty to work. No work, no pay. That was how they lived, and oft-times starved.

Sensing the warmth of the shadows, I bade farewell to my ghosts, gently knocked out the ashes from my pipe and, gripping my briefcase tightly, entered the building to begin what was to be the last chapter of my working life.

I had other duties from time to time, but I was mostly on development work, which meant I was on the site almost before a sod was turned. This had great advantages for all of us. The general foreman and I would walk the site with the local sanitary inspector, checking the sizes and types of pipes to be used and how they would link up into the main sewage system, if there was one. The rapid advent of large numbers of new houses caused us all a certain amount of teething problems – especially in regard to house sewerage and its misuse by unsuspecting people who thought that, once they pulled the chain in that jiffy, all their worries were in the

Liffey. For instance, a lot of young working couples used disposable nappies – only they disposed of them down the loo, causing a lot of chokes in their sewerage systems. Also, when both parents were working, chips often appeared to be the easiest and quickest way to fill a dinner plate. Nothing wrong with that; I've eaten my fair share of chips in my time. But when the newly untrained housewife, living, as was often the case, many miles from her mother, finished with the chip-pan, she invariably poured the used oil down the kitchen sink, where it cooled and hardened in the small four-inch pipes – which meant that the Sanitary Services men had to use a large corkscrew to unblock the system. So, while the byelaws allowed the sewerage lines of the first two houses on a block of eight to be made of four-inch pipes, due to the constant blockages the powers that be had to upgrade all drains to six-inch pipes.

Another thing we in the County Council had to do was abolish broad traps. These originated in England, which has always been the home of engineering. When they came to design the underground sewerage system in London, the English, remembering the Black Death, decided to place a very large broad trap – or intercepting trap, as it's sometimes called – at the mouth of each city borough, so that, if there was ever a recurrence of the plague, the broad trap would stop any infected matter from passing through and spreading the disease. With the passage of time, most local councils all over Britain and here in Ireland, no doubt encouraged by pipe manufacturers, came to feel the need to use these broad traps in house drains; in fact, the byelaws stipulated that they should be used in this way. But, again, people's misuse of their drains made broad traps a costly liability, with the men from Sanitary Services often having to dig up a garden and remove the trap.

Over the twenty-one years I spent working as an Inspector in Building Control, I saw many changes and new methods in the art of house-building. Mostly it was a very rewarding job; and, as standards improved, relationships between us and the builders became almost cordial. This was due to the fact that most trades were on piece-work, so it was in both the builders' and our interest to make sure standards did not drop. I can safely say that the overall standard of the building industry in the county of Dublin is very high, compared to the standards in some other countries, and I would like to think that our department helped to make it so. Over the years it was staffed by very dedicated people – engineers, building inspectors, draughtsmen and administrative staff – who happily shared their vast knowledge with one another and really went out of their way to help you if you had a problem.

Sometimes this could not have been said of the department in those earlier days when we newcomers were only finding our feet. I remember once a builder was using what I really believed were inferior sewage pipes, and I made him take them up. After a lot of shouting and cursing, he got in touch with the pipe manufacturers and they agreed to a site meeting the next day. Things looked serious for me. The next morning, I reported to my bosses what had happened and why I had condemned the pipes. They immediately agreed that what I had done was right; but when I asked for backup in the form of a senior engineer, I was told that sending an engineer out would only undermine my authority. In other words, they were saying, in the nicest possible way, that Pontius Pilate was very much alive and still washing his hands.

As 1990 was ushered in, I suddenly realised that I had only two more years before I became an old-age pensioner. At first it was a upsetting thought; but then, reflecting on it, I realised that I had had a full and very rewarding life – especially when I thought of all those young men with whom I had worked and played and shared wonderful moments. They were long dead and forgotten.

Also, I had to admit to myself that I was fast becoming a bit of a dinosaur, especially in the workplace. We had moved again, this time to Liffey House; and things had changed dramatically with the introduction of new office equipment, especially these newfangled computers, whose workings were completely over my balding head.

When Danny Gallagher and I first went into Building Control, we had been advised to join the local government union. This we did, forming our own chapter. To do so, we both had to go over to Cuffetown to get a clear card; and I had never gone back. In the 60s I had heard it had been taken down, stone by stone, for road-widening. The stones were individually numbered, and today they lie in some yard, forgotten. A sign of the times: in this computer age, even our heritage ends up as just numbers.

In 1988 I had heard that the bricklayers' union had amalgamated with the National Woodworkers. I asked whether the ceremony where a young boy held a lighted candle while being indentured to his master was still continued, and they said no. It appears that practice was done away with years before the members got rid of the name of the Ancient Guild of Incorporated Brick and Stonelayers' Union. But, even though the present-day young bricklayers seem to have no regard for tradition and for the generations of men who passed through Cuffetown's hallowed hall, if you were to pass down Cuffe Street on a dark night – as I did recently – and if you were to stop and listen with your heart, I'm certain you would still hear, above the roar of the modern-day traffic, the ring of an old brickie's trowel.

On the last day of November in the year 1992, as I said good-bye to my colleagues and friends in Building Control, I knew that the journey of this journeyman had at last come to an end; and I thanked my God for the many and varied comrades who had helped me on that journey.

The old man stood before the gates,
His head was bent and low.
Not even looking up, he muttered,
'Where, oh, where do I go?'
'What have you done,' Saint Peter asked,
'To justify your entrance here?'
'Well, I've been a bricklayer all my life,
And that's nigh sixty year.'
Opening up the gates with haste,
He gently rang his bell.
'Step inside, my dear old man,
You've had your bloody hell.'

Dame Street, Dublin. (Courtesy of The Irish Historical Picture Company.)